Dancing Girls

GERALDINE M. NORTH

Book cover taken from a hooked rug made by the author, based on an illustration by Swedish painter Elsa Beskow

Cover photograph by Lisa West,
The North Moon Photography
College Station, Texas

Dancing Girls

Short Stories

ISBN: 978-1-934582-89-3

Library of Congress Control Number: 2026908967

Published by Back Channel Press
Portsmouth, NH
Salem, NH

Printed in the United States of America

For Bill,

Simon and Alison,

and for my brother Huon

who shares my memories

Contents

"It actually doesn't take much to be considered a difficult woman. That's why there are so many of us."

Jane Goodall

The Irish Boy

You recognized the shadow on the footpath as yours by the cast of your head, the float of your dress. Sometimes your shadow stretched far beyond the cracks in the pavement at your feet and you owned your world. That's how it happened when Tommy Madison turned the corner of South Street, and your shadow brushed the toes of his red high-top sneakers.

Tommy Madison was the Irish boy, newly come to the school, accent and all: blond hair, blue-eyes and a mouth that curved up. He seemed poised for a joke, for a spot of mischief. He was unlike the tight-lipped boys in your family who had no humor, no lightness. Your family was full of rules. God was always watching, though under the blankets at night you shut Him out, along with your father who was probably God on earth.

But that last day of class when you were coming home from school, you saw Tommy's red sneakers and your shadow darkening them. You smiled, all your ten years revealed by the upward tilt of your chin and the gap between your front teeth.

Then your two older brothers came down the footpath with their three best friends. They pushed Tommy off the curb, cursing at him. “Get on home, Limey, we don’t want you here.” Your oldest brother, Lennie, brushed by you and said, “Standing on the street corner like this, you look like one of those.” And even at your age you knew what “those” meant.

One of the boys said, “What’s with your kid sister and the Limey?”

Your other brother, Carl, pointed at you. “Next time you stick with one of your own, Stacey, you hear me?”

Then the boys were off down the street, and you heard their laughter.

You wanted to pull Tommy to his feet, apologize for your brothers and their friends but you couldn’t. You watched as Tommy gathered up his schoolbooks, red-cheeked. If your brothers had seen you touch his hand, they’d know that Tommy was special to you. He was a good Irish Catholic, and Catholics weren’t welcome in our town. All hell might break loose if they mentioned *that* at the dinner table. Your brothers’ laughter would cause you shame with your father sitting in his place at the head, knife and fork in his big hands. Being the youngest you weren’t given room to talk at the table though the brothers talked with him, and he swallowed the words along with his beef and potatoes. Mother hovered, first at the stove, next at the sink, transferring food from pots to plates, tea towel over her shoulder.

Tommy Madison was different. His father bought the farm when old Masters died, and Tommy milked their two Jersey cows before school. Theirs was the only small farm left in town. One morning he called out to you as you walked by the farm. You saw his blue sweater first, then his arm waving. "Come on in!" he shouted. "Plenty of time!"

He swung the milk bucket as you walked toward the coolness of the barn. The cows were in place, tails swishing, heads in their mash. He set to, bucket between his legs.

"You ever milked before?" he asked.

"No." The cow's udder looked fit to burst.

He took your hand and showed you how to draw the milk down. His hand was smooth, not like your brothers' hands with their scrapes and scratches. You laughed together as the milk sprayed into the bucket. The barn was dappled with shadows.

"Here," he said. "Let me finish." And you stood while he finished up and the bucket was filled with frothy milk, the smell rich and creamy. "You wait for me, yeah?" he said. "We'll walk to school together."

He walked in silence, so you listened to the cicadas and watched the shadows dodging in and out of the leaves. His schoolbag swung from his shoulder, and you heard the rub of it against his hip. You wanted to walk past the school gates, past the yellow bus fumes, maybe down to the creek where dragonflies skimmed the water.

Saturday came. You had errands to run for your mother with a kitchen list to take to Mackie's Store and two string bags to bring things home. You saw his blue sweater heading down to the front gate of old Masters' farm.

"You going somewhere?" he called. His hair was bleached white in the sunlight.

"Shopping!"

"You want some company?" He vaulted the front gate, one hand on the top rail the other held out for balance. You thought of the hawk you'd seen down by the three trees, wings spread, catching the wind, beautiful in flight.

"Sure." You made space for him. Your shadows moved ahead, not touching, but forming and reforming on the stony road.

You found your stride. He threw a stone and hit a black-scabbed wattle tree, and you laughed. The trunk of the tree was thin, so you knew it was a lucky shot and you thought, on that perfect day, that luck was with him.

Early Sunday morning exhaust smoke plumed from the police car outside your house and your newly released chickens scattered. Chief Henderson waited in his car for your father to come outside.

You were finishing breakfast, cleaning up your plate with the last of the toast. Your father buttoned his coat, pulled on his boots. "Something's happened," he said. "Chief's here."

As he opened the back door you were out of your seat and quick to slip through. You sat on the cold top step knowing deep in your bones trouble lay ahead. If your brothers had been caught doing mischief you hoped the hand of the law was mightier than the hand of your father.

"Morning, Herb."

"What can I do you, Chief?"

"Madison's boy didn't come home last night." Chief Henderson opened the cab door but stayed in the cruiser. His words carried clear on the chill morning air.

Your father stepped down the three concrete steps, pausing

on each one. You saw he was thinking. "Something happen?"

Chief Henderson's breath shadowed his face. "Bert Madison says things haven't been good for the boy lately. Seems there's been trouble at school." Over the humming of the car's motor, you heard everything, "Your boys know anything about that?"

If you didn't move, they wouldn't see you. You sat on the concrete step and wondered at your brothers' muck-covered boots dropped in the entryway.

Your father stopped in the soft dust of the yard. "I'd know if my boys had done wrong, Chief." He pulled his knitted cap from his coat pocket. "So, what's happened, you think?" He settled the cap down over his ears.

"Seems some kids were partying at Lincoln Park last night and there was a ruckus. Boys say Tommy Madison left before it was over." The Chief turned off the motor and stepped out of the car. "Seems your boys left around the same time."

Before your father could speak, your mother opened the back door where you knew she'd been listening. "You have time for coffee, Chief?"

Your father didn't acknowledge her presence.

"No, Ma'am," Chief Henderson stood with his hand on the door. He took off his hat, and you thought how polite he was and how strange it was for your mother to interrupt the men's conversation.

"There's trouble?" Her skirt brushed the side of your face as she stepped past you. She placed her hand on your father's back. "You need to talk to the boys?" She was shorter than your father, but her shoulders were broader.

The Chief held his hat in his hands. "Your boys. Ma'am? They home?"

"Went out last night and came home early." Your mother's

voice was firm.

But you knew your brothers came home late after the early morning light was becoming clear at your window. You heard them on the stairs and surely your parents heard their clatter, their heavy breathing.

"We'll send them down, Chief, after they've had breakfast." Your father took your mother's arm. He half turned on the top step. "Down to the station you said?"

"There's more, Herb. We found the boy." Chief Henderson put on his hat. "Found him back in the cow shed at the farm. Beaten up." The Chief settled into the cruiser's seat. "Cows were waiting to be milked. Father found him near dead among the animals." He pulled the cruiser door closed. "Need to talk to all the boys who were at the party. Get their stories straight."

"Beaten, you say?"

"He's in the hospital," the Chief said. "We're waiting to hear news."

You wanted to move but couldn't. You knew to be silent. You'd seen your brothers push Tommy down on the street. Heard the jeering, *Limey-boy! Go on home, Pope-lover!* You remembered the hawk, wings spread, drifting on the wind currents over the three trees.

Your mother waited for the cruiser to leave the yard before she said to your father, "Come and finish your breakfast. Eggs will be cold." You were at the table when your mother grabbed your arm, and her fingers found your skin. "You go get them up, Stacey, you hear me. Tell them to come down. Now!"

You ran up the narrow wooden stairs, heart pounding with

questions. You pulled the bedclothes off your brothers. Lennie lay on his back with his arms stretched above his head; Carl was on his stomach with his dark hair fanned on the pillowcase. "Get up! Mother says, get up now!" Their clothes were piled on the floor so you nearly tripped on them when you turned back for the bedroom door.

Lennie ran down the stairs within seconds. Carl was close behind, still struggling to pull on his shirt. Your father left the toast on his plate and strode to the back entry. He stopped them in the doorway and pointed to their muck-stained boots.

"Your boots, boys?" Your father's voice rose. "Look at them!" Lennie swiveled, his eyes wide. Carl ran into him, turning.

The sausages were frying in the skillet and you saw your mother freeze. The word *boots* hung in the air. You and your mother were waiting. Your father had recognized the cow muck on the boys' boots, and everyone knew the Madisons were the only ones with a cow barn.

Your father caught Lennie by the arm and grabbed Carl by his shirt front. "Were you the ones beat up the boy?" Your father shook them both like you'd seen a dog shake a dead rabbit, the rabbit loose and broken.

You were in your chair, and as the voices rose, you slid under the tablecloth, safe among the toast crumbs on the floor. You held your knees while their voices rose and fell. Your mother slammed down the frying pan. One of the brothers yelped like a smacked puppy. There was a scuffle of feet and fists and you wanted to cover your ears. You heard your parents, the back and forth of what should be said, what should be done.

You heard your brothers' boots thrown around, then your father shouted, "Where were you both last night?"

"We came home," Lennie said. "We came home in good time."

Lennie spoke for them both, always had.

Carl was silent. You knew his silence told it all.

You thought it wasn't fair if the boys got off. Hadn't you been smacked hard for telling a lie about the little box of chocolates you stole from Emmett's shop? Your mother sent you out to the back apple tree for a switch and then she held your arm tight to the bone as she walloped your bare legs.

"You get upstairs and get dressed. We're going to the Station."

"What will you tell him?" It was your mother's voice.

"First up, we clean their boots." It was your father's God-voice and no one argued with that. You could imagine his shadow falling clear across your brothers and out to the muck-covered boots in the entryway.

"Stacey," he called. "Get out from under there and go clean your brothers' boots. Now. Clean them good!"

The River Path

Rosie Flynn cleaned the Anderson's house on Thursdays, every week like clockwork, even on days when her energy lagged or the headaches came. But today was different. Her husband, Harold, had left early to finish town work before the rain came. "Has to be done," Harold said as he bent to tie his bootlaces. He worked in culverts and drains and busted water pipes. He was older than Rosie by ten years, but he'd waited for her, gone to church and watched her sing in the choir, waited through her father's dying. He waited until she was ready, until she thought she loved him, and then they settled into his house on the Ridge where the line of hemlocks shielded their two-bedroom house. He was a good man, aware of his place in the town and the value of a working wife.

"Supper at six," Rosie called to the back of his barn coat. She tidied the kitchen and rather than waiting for the 9 a.m. church chimes, she left for the Anderson house. She had cleaned the house regularly for more than three years, and when Nina was ill last November, she had done their weekly wash and cooked some meals.

Rosie came from a long line of housecleaners: her mother, her grandmother, aunts and cousins. It was a family trade. Thanksgiving dinners were spent comparing cleaning products and ways to make a bed. Rosie had learned well. She made a nice little business for herself through the years, picking up and putting away, closing cupboard doors left open, bathrooms and bedrooms yielding up their little secrets. Not that Rosie pried, but she saw things as she cleaned. She knew who was drinking too much; what prescriptions the town pharmacy was filling and what was coming from the Chinese herbalist down by the railway yard.

The Anderson's house sat on a nice rise of lawn, with a macadam driveway and a circular garden set around a broad weeping crabtree. Rosie had arrived a half hour before she was due, and a white van sat in the driveway with *Handyman-Call Raymond Harris* printed in splashy blue letters across the sides. Nina Anderson and Raymond Harris were together at the front door. Raymond was leaving and Nina was still in her plush dressing gown when Rosie knew it was late enough for her to be dressed.

Rosie dropped the car keys into her cardigan pocket. "I'm a little early, Nina. Okay if I start?" She came to the front steps as Raymond stepped down.

"Hallo Rosie," he said, reaching to touch her arm in passing. Rosie moved quickly up the steps beyond his hand. She couldn't look at him, couldn't bear his sharp-eyed gaze.

Nina held the door open for Rosie. "Thanks a lot, Ray. You've been so helpful."

"Any time Nina. Just call me." Raymond adjusted his cap and waved.

"Kitchen sink's playing up." Nina retied the sash on her dressing gown. "And look at the time. I'll let you get on with it Rosie, I've errands to do."

Nina's husband, James, left for work at daybreak, down to the local supermarket where he was floor manager. It was a good paying job. And here was Raymond Harris, single and busy, busy, running here and there, ready to fix all the household problems the husbands were too busy to do for themselves. Raymond did a bit of everything, and Rosie smiled at the thought: yes indeed, whatever was there for him.

Rosie usually started cleaning in the Anderson's kitchen, but today she wanted to know if her eyes were telling the story right, so she carried her cleaning basket into the bedroom and there was the untidy mound of bedclothes, the pillows where no head should be, the quilt dragging. Rosie dusted the little porcelain figures, the silver-backed hairbrush. She pulled up the window shade and smacked a cluster fly buzzing in the corner.

"Are you done in here?" Nina stood at the bedroom door, a mug of coffee in her hand. "I have to shower."

"I'll make the bed later then." Rosie picked up her basket and moved into the kitchen. Stove, fridge, breakfast table, ledges where potted plants dropped their dead leaves. She polished the big dining room table with its eight chairs. And a fine table Nina sets, Rosie thought, for all the supermarket bigwigs, local government men and their wives. What would it be like to know important things before they got told in the newspaper? Harold said James Anderson could run for mayor, but Rosie reckoned he was safer where he was: knowing all the town's business and never being held responsible.

Nina came down the hall and gathered up her little black shoulder purse. She was off to have her hair permed and her nails done. Dressed for Main Street with a little too much color on her cheeks.

"I'll finish up in the next hour," Rosie said. "Enjoy yourself."

"Moneys on the table," Nina called as she closed the front door. She was known to be restless, with no children, and a house with a wide-front verandah. She rocked out there in the afternoons, her chair squeaking along with the music she played, a glass in her hand. Nina was young. Needs to keep busy, Rosie thought; busy keeps the demons at bay, and shouldn't every woman bound to her house and shining floors understand that?

Saturday came and Rosie was in the seats while her husband, newly elected captain of the local baseball team, covered third base. James Anderson was pitching for the town team. When he threw a strike out there was a burst of clapping and cheering. Young Pete Bean, umpire for the day, raised his hand and Harold signaled his pleasure.

Rosie placed her empty coffee mug on the trestle table set up behind the green wire fence that separated the playing field from the cornfield beyond. A ball hit beyond the boundary, a well-earned homer was celebrated and the local children were sent off to locate the ball from among the cornstalks. Rosie smiled at the Bartlett twins, forty years old and broad in the hips, charged with dispensing coffee, plates of blueberry muffins and lemon slices. She declined politely when Tessa Bartlett offered her another muffin. She walked the length of chairs, nodding to those she knew, a wave here and a wave there. Observing the courtesies was rewarded in small-town life and Rosie knew it was seen as a measure of character, a means of securing work.

Raymond's van was in the parking lot, but Nina and the handyman were nowhere to be seen. Rosie guessed that while James Anderson was pitching his heart out his wife was with the handyman. They'd be down by the river, on the narrow path along the bank where the grass was brown and waiting for rain. She wondered if Raymond had thought of taking a blanket. Probably not, for who thinks of practical things when your mind is on breasts and thighs and the weight of another?

Rosie flushed. She remembered that moment of simple foolishness when she met Raymond beside the river six months ago. It happened quite by accident, or that's how she later set the memory in her mind, though she often wondered if Raymond might have followed her there. She'd seen him walking toward the river path. She was taking the shortcut home and paused to watch some town boys playing kickball along the path, dodging, laughing, until the ball rolled into the river, and they waded in to retrieve it. They were still laughing at the bend of the path when Raymond called to her.

"Why, hallo Rosie," he'd said. "You waiting for me?" She was never sure if she deliberately slowed her pace to pick the wildflowers she didn't need. He caught her arm and there was the smell of him, the heat. She couldn't believe the sudden wanting in her body, the curiosity she felt in knowing what Raymond did with the other women.

She pulled away and he smiled a broad warm smile. He took her hand again and drew her into the deeper brush. He knew what he was doing, and quick as that, his hand was in her hair, pulling her down. She didn't resist. It had been a long time since someone wanted her in that way, someone practiced, who knew what a woman needed. The coat he'd been wearing wasn't thick enough to shield her from the humps of grass or to cover the shame after they were done.

She heard the boys' voices. She realized they were coming back down the path, she could hear the *thump, thump* of the ball. Raymond put his finger on his lips, and they lay there with only the sound of their breathing. Rosie prayed the boys wouldn't knock the ball into the bushes, while beside her, Raymond laughed. "We're safe," he whispered.

He was enjoying this moment, the excitement of hiding, the possibility of being discovered. But Rosie realized the stupidity of it, the thought of Harold knowing, of having to explain, watching his face.

She never told Harold. She would never let herself think of Raymond in that way again. Everyone held their secrets tight in a small town, but sometimes, when she arrived to clean one of her client's houses and the white van was leaving, she felt a pang, a shiver down her legs. Never again, Rosie thought, never again, ever.

A cheer rose from the stands. James Anderson had struck out someone. It seemed the home team would win so Rosie decided to stay through the final innings. She knew Harold would be in fine spirits that night. As captain of the winning side, they might be invited to the Anderson's for supper along with the town selectmen and mayor. What was she thinking? Not among the Anderson's friends, not when she cleaned their houses. Harold wouldn't accept any invitation from them anyway, not after

James Anderson had lobbied to be team captain, and Harold had won the position by two votes. It was close, Harold had said, and there were some hard feelings after.

"The Anderson's house helps provide for us," Harold said at the time. "That's the way of it, Rosie; there's them and there's us."

Rosie checked for Raymond's white van, and it was still there in the parking lot, though he was nowhere to be seen. Rosie buttoned her cardigan against the afternoon breeze.

There was one other time, several weeks ago, when Raymond came about the roof shingles. Harold had seen the green moss gathering along the edges of the roof. "Not good, Rosie," he'd said. "We'll have to call Ray." And Raymond came in his white van, sleeves rolled to his elbows, hair slicked back from his forehead. He brought his ladder and deftly went about the job. Rosie heard him moving over the roof, heard all the small movements, the scratch and scrape of the work. She listened, tea towel in her hand, breakfast dishes waiting to be dried.

"Jobs finished, Rosie," he said as he came to the back door. "Work makes you thirsty." He was sure of himself, comfortable in his body, at ease in his world. He wore khakis so the dirt didn't show. His tool belt was slung low on his hips, and he wiped his boots on the outside mat before he came into the house.

"A glass of water, and thanks, Rosie." Her hand touched his hand as he took the glass, and Rosie knew he was waiting for her response. *Never again, she thought, not ever again.*

Rosie refilled the glass. She was wearing an old summer dress, too short now to wear in town. Her legs were still good; her waist hadn't thickened like her mother's had at her age. She watched Ray's eyes and smelled his cologne. Before she could take back the empty glass, she heard her husband's car on the driveway.

Rosie wasn't expecting Harold, not during a workday, and she wondered briefly if he suspected something. She braced her body against the kitchen cabinet.

"Just needed to check how bad it was, Ray." Harold came through the kitchen door. "Thought you might find some rot up there." He put his arm around the handyman's shoulders and led him outside. Rosie listened to their voices. She heard her husband say, "So, what do I owe you, Ray?"

Rosie rinsed the glass and set it to drain. Harold knew the handyman, knew what he might be after when he finished a job, but he didn't know it all, didn't really know his Rosie.

The baseball game was over. Harold was rising to accept the battered silver cup for his team. There were clapping and wordy speeches, followed by more cheering and slapping of backs. There was laughter over dropped balls and missed bases. Rosie saw Harold holding the silver cup high above his head, the back of his shirt wet with sweat, his hair needing a trim. And instead of thinking about Harold's hair and where she'd put the scissors, her mind strayed to the riverbank. Raymond had a feral something. He left it like a calling card after he'd fixed the faucet, put up the new shelves or cleaned the gutters; left it for the woman at home who longed again for a heated moment. Keep busy, she thought, busy, busy, because when Raymond came to fix the roof, she might have said *yes*, had Harold not come home she might have followed him off.

Harold caught her by her arm. "So, what did you think, Rosie?" He was laughing, captain of the winning side. "Great game! Wasn't James in fine form?" He led her toward their car, talking and talking, arm around her waist. She noticed the white van was gone. Small-town living was like a game of poker, sometimes winning, sometimes losing, but always shielding your cards from the other players.

Her shoe caught in the rough grassy field, and she would have fallen had she not clung to her husband.

"You okay, Rosie?" Harold asked. "You tired or something?"

My Mother Explained Sex

Wouldn't you know it? My mother explained sex to me the day after I first had it. I mean, she finally told me our Basset hound was pregnant because she, the hound, had hung out with the male Beagle down the street.

"You know," my mother said. "They've *come together,*" and she sort of wrinkled her nose, and added, "Now poor Trixie has to deal with the outcome."

Come together. My mother is a Puritan from way back and maybe that's why there's only me. Her words echoed in my ears, and I thought of Joey and me in the back of his family's station wagon last night, coming together in a haze of curiosity, of fumbling lips and knocking heads. Sure, it was sex, but it wasn't anything like I'd seen on HBO.

I was curious, all right? The mechanics of it all.

Joey wore a condom, just like we were advised to do in Sex Ed, so I hoped I wasn't going to suffer like Trixie, you know, pregnant and all. I'm sixteen, legal age, and Joey's a bit older. I'm not sure I even like him but he's practiced. You know how word gets about. And he's good looking in a way, cute haircut and T-shirts that are a little too tight. He works out, plays football on the weekends and drives his parents' station wagon. That last is a plus.

His father teaches the Sex Ed course at the high school, so that gives Joey some creds, and makes everyone think Joey knows everything. He seems a methodical boy, but can he keep a secret? Afterwards I began to worry, once the rush was over and I was home in my room. I wanted to call Missy, my BFF, but I needed to think things through, get a good night's sleep.

"Did you enjoy the film?" my mother called as I ran up the stairs.

What film? I'd forgotten that was my excuse for going out with Joey. It was "Jurassic Park" on the big screen, surround sound, lots of noise and the music loud enough to deafen you. I knew the story so that wasn't a problem but maybe Mum's friends were there. The theater isn't that large and you see everyone coming and going. Just have to hope, really. One step at a time.

That's what Missy said, when I finally confided in her. "Take it a week at a time, Pammy, I'm sure you'll be okay."

It was her tone of voice that shook me. She didn't lecture me or ask for details, she seemed to be sorry for me. "Joey?" she said after we'd walked the hall between Math and Social Studies. "You mean, Joey Carter? Why him?" I shushed her but she went on. "He's such a loser, Pammy."

That surprised me. She was my best friend so I told her why I chose him and she agreed that Joey's dad would have spoken to him, you know, teaching sex and all. I mean you go to your best friend when you have some problem to talk about, don't you?

Although Miss Parsons, my English teacher, says you have to talk to your parents if you have any life questions: "They're the best models you have." And I thought, all I have is my mum who's into dogs and baking cookies for the Girl Scouts, of which I'm not a member.

But my second-best friend, Prue, is a Girl Scout and she's going for the Eagle badge, that's her thing, learning how to tie knots and put up a tent and dig a trench for a toilet. I said to her, "Prue, if that's all you're going to learn what are you going to do the rest of your life?" She punched my arm and said, "Wake up, Pammy, there's a big, wonderful world out there." Prue is younger than me by six months but at times she seems older. Maybe because her dad left home soon after she was born, and her mum was left to cope with a baby and get a job like my mum had to do. I confided in Prue because she's such a good scout, and because she's a really good person, too. She looked concerned and asked if I was sure I was okay and if I should see a counselor or someone adult.

Which brings me to Gran, who I still like, and who took us in when dad left. She wasn't old then, but she wasn't young either, and I had to sit up straight at the table and keep my room tidy while mum went to work at the local vet's because she's always loved dogs, any four-legged creature, really. It's the two-legged ones that give her migraines. It's not that mum didn't love me but she just didn't have time for me and my constant questions. It was Gran who listened to me and put Band Aids on my scrapes and made sure I had supper most nights, but she's too old to talk to about sex.

Funny thing about high school is that you can attend all the classes, stay awake, and sit up in the chair, even hand in all your assignments, but never learn about the important things. I realized that when I watched television. I didn't know where Sudan was, or Tasmania, or about the aurora borealis in the northern hemisphere with its fantastic shapes and fabulous colors. It's where the Innuit live. And I learned about fungi and edible mushrooms from the Science Channel and that bees wax is a natural disinfectant. And you watch all the sexy scenes on TV and still wonder about the mechanics of it.

Sex with Joey wasn't like you see on the movies or like you read about in those books where the pages fall open at a certain point in the story. So, I was relieved to pull on my clothes and hear the engine start. We were off the back road, parked in a little side path. Not a place I knew, but Joey seemed to know it and I wondered if I really was, like he said, the first girl he'd brought there. Mum had told me, "Even the nicest boys try it." Well, Joey wasn't the nicest boy in the school and the good boys only wanted to hold my hand and be friends, so you could say my curiosity won out.

Friends like Missy and Prue are special but trusting them with my newfound knowledge had been a tricky decision. I wasn't sure I should have spilled all the details. Whether Missy might blab or not. I knew Prue would honor her scout oath, but Missy? School does funny things to friendships. You can have a friend one day and lose them on another. It all depends on the bus you catch, the team you're on, the class you're in, but Missy and I have been close since kindergarten. Her mother and mine are both divorced, both work, both go to the same church on Sundays. I swore her to secrecy, even though I've seen enough stories on HGTV to know that people have a hard time keeping secrets.

Mum's taking Trixie into the vet to check her out today. To see if the Beagle down the road left his seed behind, whether Trixie is indeed pregnant. You hear all sorts of stories about condoms and whether they're really safe, you know, pinholes and old latex. But they're in our bathrooms at school and I've seen the janitor changing up those packets regularly, so I guess everything's okay.

It's the waiting that's getting me down. I'm worried and then I'm not. I learned the mechanics of sex but I'm only now figuring out what it all means. Another week or so and I can relax, meanwhile I'll take it one day at a time, get on with my homework, and finally see Jurassic Park with my BFF, Missy.

Two Girls on a Wall

Lacey pushed her shopping cart down the supermarket aisle, past the shelves of spinach and green kale and stopped at the fruit bins. She would make a peach pie for the family tonight before she left for nursing school. Lacey was in her final year of training, four years in the city, independent and grown apart from her hometown. She was ready to move on when she saw an old high school friend working on the apple bins.

"Hey Meg, how are you doing?" Lacey saw Meg had put on weight.

"Lacey?" Meg dropped the apples in her hand. "It's been so long!"

Meg put her hand on the blue apron stretched tight on her rounded belly. "Look," she said. "I'm having a baby."

"Congratulations!" Lacey said. Meg's hair was lifeless. "Who's the lucky fellow?"

Lacey bagged the peaches. Her mother should have told her. In high school, she and Meg had planned big weddings to handsome men their fathers would admire. Then they weren't friends, and after graduation, Lacey enrolled in nursing school and Meg took a job at the local supermarket where she wore heels and bright lipstick.

"Five months." There was no ring on her finger. "We're getting married, Brian and me." Meg smiled but her eyes were dull. An older woman pushed past Lacey, and their carts scraped against each other. Lacey steadied her cart and dropped the peaches into her bag.

Once when she and Meg were in high school and walking down Main Street together Brian drove by. "Looking good, girls!" he had called out, maybe with a whistle, a wave. "You want a smoke?"

Lacey remembered how Meg slid one from the packet and how she had reached for one, too. He lit both their cigarettes, and they inhaled together. Meg let the smoke drift from her open mouth while Lacey had a coughing fit.

"You have to practice." Meg had said and inhaled again.

Back then, Lacey had wondered about going out with Brian. Maybe it was his convertible, the easy way he smoked unfiltered, the way his elbow rested on the open window, his easy way with the girls. Their high school days were another life. It was old news, an old story. In another year she will have a diploma. The city was two hours away and there were jobs begging to be filled.

Lacey pushed her cart closer to the fruit bins. The supermarket smelled of rotting leaves and over-ripe fruit. She bagged a bunch of purple grapes. "I didn't know you and Brian were getting married."

Meg carried her box of fruit discards to the bin of brown-skinned pears. She studied them for a moment before quickly picking out the bruised ones. "It doesn't seem real," she said. "For months it hasn't seemed real." She pushed her cart to the next bin where the melons were stacked. "Brian says it'll work out."

"You have a wedding date?"

Meg picked up a small green melon and examined it. "Brian has to get time off." There was no red nail polish, her blouse needed ironing. "You know he's still working at Midas."

They all knew Brian was no good. Should she tell Meg he picked her up just yesterday, the intimacy of his arm, the invitation to the Drive-in? He had backed up with the side window down and a smile on his face. "Well, hallo stranger, drive you home?"

Brian steered with one hand. A packet of cigarettes bulged in his shirt pocket and he saw her looking. "You want one?" He smelled of oil and gas and cigarettes.

"No, thanks," she said. "Given them up."

When he stopped at her front gate, he leaned across her body to open the car door, and his arm pressed against her chest. "Come to the Drive-in with me this Saturday?" he asked, cigarette between his lips.

It was lunchtime, the supermarket was humming. Lacey wanted to get away from the despair in Meg's eyes. They had never been real friends, just high school kids who did things together for a time and shared each other's secrets.

"Are you okay?" Lacey asked.

"I just need a friend to talk to, you know, just talk." Meg was standing quite still with her hands on the box of discarded fruit. "Lacey," her voice trailed off. "I don't have the money." Her voice wavered.

There was desperation in Meg's voice, but Lacey had left high school behind, left Meg behind. She wanted a hot shower, and a cup of her mother's green tea. "I'm leaving tomorrow. Gotta finish packing."

Meg's face flushed. "Of course, Lacey, I'm sorry, I know you're busy." Meg lifted the bin of discards and moved across the aisle to the vegetable section where the small potatoes were bundled in plastic bags.

"See you round, Meg." Lacey headed for the exit.

That night after supper with her family, the phone rang. Lacey was drying her hair. The supper dishes were washed and put away and their favorite show was coming on TV.

"It's Meg. Can we talk?" Meg still lived with her mother, who worked at the dry cleaners on Maple Avenue. Lacey remembered that Meg's grandmother lived with them, and she was old and frail and didn't like visitors, especially Meg's friends coming around.

"You want to meet tonight?" Lacey could hear paper rustling, a bump as though something had dropped on the floor. "Now?"

Meg was breathing hard as if she'd been running. "I have to talk to someone," she said. "I have to make a decision."

"This about the wedding?" Lacey threw the damp towel over the back of a chair. "I've just washed my hair, Meg, I'm really tired."

Lacey's mother looked up with a face and mouthed, *who's calling*? Her father coughed. Her sister was curled up on the sofa waiting to watch the show with her.

The line buzzed. "It's too late, Meg, can we meet tomorrow? Coffee at the Corner Café round ten?" There was a pause. Lacey thought Meg had hung up. "You still there?" she asked.

It was the last year of high school when Lacey and Meg went to the Corner Café to buy sodas and donuts and hang out on stools by the big side window overlooking the Midas shop. Meg watched Brian working at the counter and Barbara joined them because she had a crush on Tony who also worked there. Meg and Barbara became close friends, and they didn't call Lacey anymore.

"Is there someone else you can talk to? Is Barbara still around?"

"Barbara left town months ago."

Lacey ate the last of the peach tart. "I can meet you in the morning, Meg, before my bus leaves."

The line was quiet. "Okay, Lacey." Meg's voice sounded far away. "See you tomorrow."

It was all over the morning news. A man walking his dog along the beach at daybreak had seen her lying on the rocks beneath the sea wall. He said it was the orange buoy tangled in her hair that first caught his eye.

"I'm going down to the beach." Lacey pulled on her new white jacket. "I have to see for myself." She was having trouble with the zipper; her fingers weren't working properly. How was she to know Meg was so desperate.

"Friend or no friend, you be careful now," her mother said. "Don't you get involved!"

"I won't be long." She pulled up the hood of her coat and tightened her scarf. If only she hadn't washed her hair last night, if she hadn't been leaving today. Maybe if Barbara hadn't left town she could have talked to Meg and Lacey wouldn't feel so guilty.

Her mother reached out and hugged her. "Poor little Meg. Poor little baby. There is nothing you could have done."

All signs of the medics, the ambulance, had been washed away with the outgoing tide. The sand had been raked clean, and a lone police officer was posted by the steps at the far end of the pier. The sea wind was fierce, the waves slapped relentlessly against the rocks below her feet.

Lacey remembered dancing on that sea wall, high above the outgoing tide. The acceptance letter had arrived from nursing school. She was in the program. She was starting a new life. She had stood fearlessly on the sea wall and begun to dance, little steps, back and forth, a little skip, the *click, click, click* of her fingers, listening to her heels strike the old stones.

The Sword Swallower

A small traveling circus had set up on a barren lot at the edge of town where the weekend Farmer's Market was held, and I was there with my sister, Mattie, and my older brother Johnny. We were waiting in the dust and the sticky black flies for the red curtains to open on the Great Sebastian. Somewhere a crow called. There were several caravans parked along the west fence, and tents were set up in a crude circle with large placards advertising the Bearded Woman, the Snake Woman and the Strong Man with his great black beard. We had wandered through those sideshows already but it was the last tent that drew us to the front of the small, straggly crowd.

The afternoon sun threw shadows down the five steps that reached from the hard ground up to the platform of rough-cut boards to where the garish placard screamed: "Sword Swallower" in psychedelic colors. A thin girl in a green satin dress came out from behind the curtains to introduce the man, and her arm was long and pale and I held my breath as I followed her pointing finger. The Great Sebastian came through the back curtains with a flourish, a broad red sash held his belly, a shiny white turban wrapped his head. He was bare-chested and hairy and his arm muscles bulged. He owned the stage.

I stared at the great man. His moustache was as black and as neatly curled as the bright poster depicted, but his potbelly, dusty shoes, and faded red sash were poor imitations. I did not care. The sword on the table held my gaze. The blade was long and silver and reflected a reddish light, maybe from the red curtains or maybe from some power within. I didn't have time to work on that thought because he had arrived.

The Great Sebastian stepped forward and took up the sword and the afternoon sun caught the fancy gold and silver threads swinging from the handle. He swung the sword around his head, back and forth, and I heard the *swish* as it cut the air. The thin girl went behind the back curtain and we heard music like a snake charmer might play. The big man held the sword above his head with both hands and the music from behind the red curtain grew; a wheezy crescendo of pipes, accompanied by a long sigh from the audience below the stage.

"Are you ready?" the Great Sebastian asked in a deep voice, drawing out the last word so it sounded like *reeeeddy*. He looked right at us, at Mattie and me, and smiled.

"Yes!" The single word erupted from the audience and Mattie and I were caught in the promise of that word. Mattie squeezed my hand so hard I let out a cry and a woman standing behind me patted my shoulder.

"It will be alright dear," she whispered. "It's all *pretend*."

"It's just sleight of hand!" Johnny hissed in my ear and

nudged me in the back.

I wanted to believe him but I wasn't sure. The sword looked awfully sharp.

The music rose and I heard a drum roll. The Great Sebastian held the sword's shaft with both hands, and slowly, slowly, the blade disappeared into his mouth, past his tongue and down into his gullet. The hideous expectation of gushing blood made my own belly ache.

Within five seconds–I was counting fast–he pulled the sword out and swung it above his head. He cut the air with the sword once, twice, and with his head turned to watch the audience's reaction, he placed it reverently back on the table. No one moved. How supremely clean it was, that long, bright blade. No blood, no saliva dripped from the pointed end. It was a miracle. We clapped joyously at the wonder of it all.

"How'd he do it?" I asked Mattie.

"Dunno," was her answer and Mattie knows everything, she's a year older than me.

We talked about the Great Sebastian for days. How had he done it, how had he swallowed such a long sword without cutting himself? Was it a trick shaft that retracted the blade? Or did he have a gullet that was strong enough not to be cut? It was all pretend, but a very clever, practiced pretend.

That weekend Mattie and I wandered down by the wood heap where Johnny was cutting wood for our backyard barbecue. Mattie and I had put our skipping ropes aside and were sitting on upturned logs, resting drowsily in the warm afternoon. It was peaceful there where the hemlocks grew, and we watched the axe rise and fall in my brother's hand.

"It was a trick." Johnny assured us.

"But how'd he do it? Mattie asked for the umpteenth time.

"It was a trick. It wasn't a real sword. It was a fake."

"Yeah, but how fake?" I asked.

Johnny was eleven and strong and my older brother. He had all the best ideas and he knew so much more than Mattie and me. It was a warm day, we were happily relaxed, and I could hear the drone of green blowflies.

"I can show you a trick," Johnny said. He picked up the axe and moved to the chopping block. He put a piece of wood on the block and raised the axe. We waited to see the wood split in two but Johnny stopped the axe just before it reached the wood. The axe came down halfway, stopped, then swung up! The action was fluid. Amazing. He did it again. "Just like that," he said. "You expect to see one thing, but you see another."

"That was great," Mattie said.

"Put your finger there, Liz, and I'll show you the trick." Johnny pointed to the chopping block. "It's only your finger."

"You haven't practiced enough," I said. "Your tricks don't always work."

Johnny swung the axe back and forth. He looked like the woodcutter in my Grimms book just before he cut off the wolf's head and Red Riding Hood was saved. He looked like a hero standing there, and he was my brother, and I knew he was wiser than me.

"I just showed you how it's done," Johnny said.

Mattie was getting restless. "Go on Liz. I dare you."

I remembered when Johnny pretended he'd cut off his thumb, how I believed the cotton wool covered in red cochineal was his blood. The relief when I discovered the trick and how it was done. But still there was doubt.

"I don't want to," I said. Johnny's tricks didn't always work the way he said they would, like the disappearing tomato that ended up squashed all over my hankie. But he was clever with matchstick puzzles and card tricks. And he had just shown us the axe trick and how it worked, how the axe didn't strike the wood.

"Nothing will happen." Johnny held the axe with his two hands. "It's just sleight of hand, Liz, it's like magic."

"Are you sure?"

"Go on," said Mattie. "Johnny's good at tricks. He's our Great Sebastian!"

Reluctantly, I put my pointer finger on the block. It looked small and white and the nail was chewed down. I turned my head away but I saw Mattie was leaning forward, watching closely. She was all the audience Johnny needed.

My brother raised the axe. For one quick second it blocked out the sun, then the axe came down and rose again.

I felt the blade connect, a sudden jolt along and up my arm, and I couldn't breathe. I stared at the splash of blood on the tree stump where the first joint of my pointer finger lay. There was a moment of breathless silence then Johnny dropped the axe. It was dull and gray, quite unlike the shiny sword of the Great Sebastian's. Mattie began to wail. Nothing bad was supposed to happen.

I looked down at my hand and, sure enough, the first joint of my pointer finger was gone. Blood seeped from the ragged flesh. It was supposed to be Johnny's trick, a sleight of hand, a magical moment.

"What happened?" Mattie's voice was a cry of disbelief

"Wrap it up," Johnny yelled. "Mattie, get Liz to wrap it up."

Mattie was bent over. She was holding her stomach. "You shouldn't have done it, Johnny. You shouldna done it."

I pulled up the front of my T-shirt and put my bloody hand in the fold.

“It was the axe did it.” It didn’t sound like Johnny’s voice, it was high and wobbly. He flicked the tiny piece of finger off the stump and sat down on its bloody surface.

“Get off, Johnny,” Mattie shouted, pushing his shoulder. “Liz’s gotta sit down.”

“The finger,” I whispered. “Where’s my finger? Mum can put it back together if we find it.” But it was gone among the leaves and debris and chips of wood.

Johnny led me home while Mattie wailed behind us. Mother wrapped my finger in yards of bandage, all the time questioning us, admonishing us, her voice rising and falling until we gave up listening. We stayed in our bedrooms until supper-time and we didn’t try to explain the Great Sebastion’s sword trick, we knew it wouldn’t help the situation. That evening, I had a large white bandage to show my father, and his words mimicked my mother’s: Why did you do it? Who’s this Sebastian fellow? Johnny should have had more sense. What were you all thinking? On and on, until we fell asleep.

Small Brown Snail

Janet hailed the 6:20 p.m. Blue Line bus.

"Evening Miss." The driver greeted her with a cheery wave of his hand.

"Evening George." She sat on one of the double front seats facing the aisle, beside a big woman who drew in her elbows. The bus was half full and there were always a few faces she recognized and acknowledged. Sitting opposite her were two teenage girls who giggled over pictures in a *People* magazine.

Fresh out of high school, Janet had begun working at Second Read, and at thirty-five had bought the shop outright from the previous owner, a gentle man who had taught her the business. She had found in those small book-filled rooms a satisfying haven, reading for hours, interrupted only when the front doorbell rang for a customer or when she received a new allotment of used books that required cataloguing.

Janet was reading a memoir, a dog-eared paperback, *Sound of a Wild Snail Eating*, written by a woman confined to her hospital bed with a very nasty illness. A friend of the author had given her a small brown snail to put in a terrarium on her bedside table and the author, trapped in her bed, followed its daily progress. While the snail moved slowly from leaf to leaf and over the mossy soil, the sick woman kept a journal detailing its journey.

Janet also kept a journal, so she understood the woman. The ritual of capturing the minutiae of each day was a pleasure she kept for the last hour before bed. Like the snail and the woman, Janet had no place new to travel. Surrounded by piles of old books and *New Yorker* magazines, she was cloistered in her small apartment and satisfied with her predictable world.

While Janet was fully engaged in the memoir, the bus lurched around a corner and her rucksack slid off her lap. She had forgotten to zip up the bag when she had retrieved her book, and its contents spilled out across the floor between the seats. She felt exposed under everyone's startled gaze.

The big woman seated next to her let out an "Oh dear," and drew her knees together. "You need any help?" She was large and round and the buttonholes strained across her floral dress.

Janet tucked the book under her thigh. "Thank you," she said. "I can manage."

Her wallet had flopped open, her credit card had landed across the aisle; her pen had washed up against the painted sneakers of the young girl opposite. The gilhoolie she had ordered last week and just received fell with a clatter of steel on steel.

"Sorry," she said to her seat companion. "How careless of me."

The two girls across the aisle leaped into action and handed

Janet her credit card and comb. "Here," one said. "Your ballpoint?"

The other young girl bent to retrieve the gilhoolie but drew back her hand. "Oh shit," she said. "What's that for?"

"It opens cans," Janet said. "And bottle tops."

"Yeah?" The girl settled back in her seat and nudged her friend. "Never seen one like that before."

Janet picked it up. Aware of the flush in her cheeks, she stuffed everything back in her bag. The two girls repositioned their legs and opened their magazine.

The big woman turned to Janet. "Got everything, dear?"

"Thank you." She felt for her book. "Yes."

The woman stared at her rucksack and coughed. "You got a reason for keeping that ugly thing?"

"It's a gilhoolie," Janet explained. She had seen it advertised in a magazine and the word had captivated her. Such an odd word, such an old-fashioned tool.

"Never heard of it." The woman shifted her feet and sniffed. "Looks like some sorta weapon." She folded her arms on her chest. "Woman next door shoulda had one of those," she said.

Janet waited for her to elaborate.

"Woman alone," the woman repeated. "Who'd a thought."

The bus stopped and the two teenagers got off. A young man came on, swung around the metal pole, and slid into the empty seat across from Janet.

"Did something happen to her?" Janet asked. "Was she a friend?" The bus passed the Verizon store. Three more stops before she got off.

"Woman was raped." The big woman did not lower her voice.

Janet saw the young man was listening intently. She heard the *snap* of chewing gum against his tongue.

"She shoulda had one of those things." The woman moistened

her lips. "She'd had one of them," she added. "She woulda clobbered him." She sat a little straighter. "Coulda laid him out before something happened!"

Janet thought about that. The gilhoolie could open any jar, any bottle. But split open a man's head? Maybe? Maybe with enough force.

"She lived alone?" Janet asked.

"Police think he followed her home." The woman set her sturdy shoes together. Her thick stockings were beige and ribbed. "He had a knife. You see it on TV, never think it'd happen next door."

Janet glanced at the young man across the aisle. His eyes were bloodshot. Probably on drugs. He had crossed his legs and stretched them into the aisle so that passengers getting off the bus had to step over them.

Living alone did not protect you from the world, Janet thought, but it did save you from inconsequential conversations. How long could the snail live in that terrarium alone? The sick woman's world was slowly collapsing, but the snail? Janet shrugged; she was not sure that either of them could survive.

"This's my stop." The big woman stood and patted Janet's shoulder. "You keep that thing close," she said. "Never know when you might need it."

Two more stops. Janet knew the bus route by heart even when she was reading, recognized the cool rush of air each time the door opened and closed. The sameness of the trip was reassuring and she opened her book. The sick woman lying among her pillows watched the little snail and, once, when it reached the lip of the terrarium, she had used her pen to flip it back down to the soft cushion of moss.

Janet glanced at the back of the bus. There were not many

passengers left. People in the back seats were staring out their side windows; an older couple met her gaze and smiled; a young woman with long blonde hair seemed to be napping. A man with a fierce dark beard was busy with his newspaper, flapping it against the back of the empty seat in front of him.

The young man across the aisle was staring at her. "You want some company over there?"

Janet shook her head. He was obnoxious. He did not warrant a reply. He wasn't wearing socks, and his ankles were chapped above his sneakers. She saw a partial tattoo, a name above the ankle bone. Her cousin had a saying of Kahlil Gibran's tattooed up her leg. She did not like tattoos, such a nasty use of ink.

The bus stopped and the older couple walked slowly up the aisle and got off. The next stop was hers.

"Hey, Lady, look what I found!" The young man had reached across the aisle and grabbed something from behind her shoe. "This yours?" He was holding out her small leather-covered journal.

She was careful not to touch his hand.

"You a writer?" He looked at the journal and then at the book she was reading. He folded his arms across his chest. "Just being friendly. No problem then, you're busy." His rib cage showed through his tightly fitted T-shirt with its large peace symbol emblazoned in washed-out black. He sat back in his seat and stretched his legs into the aisle again.

Today she had worn her hair down, so her reflection in the darkened window behind the young man's head made her look years younger. The truth was, both she and the sick woman in her book were in their mid-forties, the same age.

The bus shuddered to a stop. Janet gathered up her rucksack and slung the leather strap across her chest. She stepped over the young man's legs, and as she reached the open door, she smiled at the bus driver.

"Good night, George," she called.

There was a sudden movement behind her. The young man was on his feet and she heard his shoes clatter on the metal steps.

As the doors of the Blue Line bus closed behind them, she heard the driver calling, "Good night, Miss, have a nice evening.

The Haberdasher's Daughter

Olivia Benton lit the first match and held it against the mannequin's sleek black hair. The flame quickly moved down the face and she watched the unblinking blue eyes melt. She had never wanted plastic mannequins with cheap nylon hair, but no, Neville had insisted, these mannequins were the most cost-effective. Tiny spirals of smoke lifted toward the ceiling. The gasoline-soaked newspapers crackled under her shoes. She threw down a lit match and scrambled out through the narrow trapdoor onto the floor of her father's haberdashery store. The smell of gasoline was overpowering. In her haste, she caught her hip against a table of bright summer shirts, and the sudden *screech* of wood on wood startled her. She needed to leave the store at once, quickly and quietly.

Neville Rutledge had arrived at Benton's Haberdashery as a

sweet-faced seventeen-year-old. He appeared in a worn sweater and scuffed shoes and asked Olivia's father if he could work there. "You can, my boy, but those clothes won't do, won't do at all." Olivia had watched her father measure Neville from top to toe, chest and waist. When she next saw Neville, he was unrecognizable in a smart new suit, white shirt and dark tie, and in those early years her father continued to dress Neville in Benton suits, and in those early novice years, just like the mannequins in the front store windows.

Olivia grew comfortable with Neville's presence. They were teenagers together. She liked the way Neville began dressing the male models in the store window, how he changed their clothes on Sunday afternoons with a sheet covering the front window for privacy. She liked the way he smiled at her when she came to visit her father and held the front door open as she came up the steps. During the school holidays, she worked in the store and waited for Neville to ask her out. She was disappointed at his lack of interest.

Her father had sold high-end clothes to the town's businessmen and political figures for more than forty years. Olivia had seen him lean over the worn front counter and while he patiently listened to his customers' concerns, he gathered in their money. As a child she had wandered the aisles and let the coat sleeves brush her hair and smelled the warm richness of fresh tweed and satin linings. On Saturday mornings, she had been allowed to organize the silk ties and cotton handkerchiefs and fold them into the narrow wooden drawers.

"Neatness," her father had told her, "is everything." She had been raised to appreciate fine cloth, well-tailored and well-fitted to compliment the most unfortunate of figures.

The years passed, and Neville was allowed to live in an apartment above the store, rent-free. It had its own outside entrance and narrow, metal staircase, and her father liked him living close by. "Having Young Neville on the premises is a godsend," her father had explained. She understood that Neville was there to open and close the shop and keep an eye on the inventory.

When her father suffered his first heart attack, Olivia had confronted him. "I know I can run things," she told him. "Neville can help me in the shop while you convalesce."

"Shop? My haberdashery business?" Her father's face had reddened. "It's been a fixture on Emerson Street since before you were born." He stood by the store's front window supported by his walker; his breathing was labored and she saw how her father had aged since her last visit.

"Everything has changed while I've been away," Olivia said. She was surprised at how many people passed the store without a second glance, the speed at which cars rounded the corner when the lights turned.

Her father's back remained ramrod straight, the dark blue suit he favored fell from his shoulders without a crease. "It's a man's world, Olivia." He pointed to the androgynous mannequins in the window. "We cater to men, dear. They don't want their inseams measured by a woman."

"Neville could take the measurements while I tend the counter, father." Olivia glanced at the rack of dark suits and neatly hung trousers. "I am your daughter," Olivia's voice was firm. "The business must stay in the family, carrying on the Benton name."

"Of course it will remain Benton's Haberdashery," her father said. "Where else would men go for their suits?" He turned his walker toward the counter. "Just be patient Olivia, I'll consult with Neville later."

While Olivia's mother was alive Neville was invited to Thanksgiving and Christmas dinners, where he sat at her father's right hand. Her mother fussed over Neville as though he was the son she didn't have, and Olivia wondered at the depth of her mother's devotion. When Olivia moved away to finish her studies in art history, she rarely came home, knowing Neville would contact her if she was needed. When her mother died and the house was sold, her father and Neville stripped the place of everything Olivia remembered, and her childhood was erased. Her father had collected a box of small items he thought she might like: her mother's diamond engagement ring, a wooden giraffe whose origins baffled her, and several small, framed family photos. Neville was present in each of them.

After her mother's funeral, her father explained he was moving into the apartment above the shop. "It's more convenient, Olivia. And I'll no longer require a car."

"But what about Neville, father? He's been there forever." Her father sat behind his desk thumbing through papers while she contemplated his balding head. "Why not buy one of the new apartments on Newell Street?"

Olivia knew the layout of the small upstairs apartment above Benton's Haberdashery: two bedrooms, a small kitchen, and a small living room where Neville had his television set. It wasn't as though her father lacked resources. He could easily afford a place in the new apartments, but her father was unmoving.

When she called for details about the store, her father said, "You need to ask Neville, dear. He knows how things are moving." She found it increasingly difficult to have any conversations with her father about the business, and it was quite impossible for her to ask Neville for details.

When she suggested modernizing the store, even in a modest

way, Neville had reminded her. "Oh, no, Miss Olivia, this is your father's haberdashery. We like it this way."

In late fall she received a brief note from Neville saying that her father was not well and she should come home, so she booked a room in a local hotel and after dinner reached the apartment above Benton's Haberdashery. At the top of the narrow stairs, Neville opened the door.

"Your father will be glad to see you, Miss Olivia." He ushered her into the sitting room, where her father sat in an overstuffed floral chair wrapped in a plaid blanket. Olivia saw how frail he had become. She saw that one bedroom had been turned into an office. The door of the other bedroom was closed.

Neville remained steadfastly by her father's side. He hired another young man to help in sales and took on more responsibility in running the business. He continued a respectful calm with the customers and a polite distance from Olivia. He made sure her father came down to the store to keep up with the local gossip, retain his influence in the town and remain the face of the store.

Throughout these changes, Olivia found her relationship with Neville irritating. The store looked a little shabby, a little old-fashioned. As her father's health declined, she asked once again if Neville might update the store and he had replied, "No, Miss Olivia. What would our customers say?"

When the business was hers, she decided, she would paint the walls, freshen up the shelves, change the flooring, and finally buy some handsome, fiberglass mannequins with real hair befitting a modern Benton's Haberdashery.

The day Jonas Willard Esq. came to the store to read her father's will, Neville arrived in an immaculate pin-striped, black Benton suit and dark tie.

"Good morning, Miss Olivia." Neville placed his black umbrella by the front door of her father's shop. "Waiting for Mr. Willard?" He called a greeting to the young man standing at the counter in an elegant store suit and quickly explained that he would not be long, then turning to Olivia, he asked, "Are you well?"

"How are you, Neville?" She took his hand. "The upstairs apartment? My father's belongings, have they been packed?"

"The boxes are ready." He stood close beside her. "We must plan for a large funeral, Miss Olivia. The Aubrey Hall has been booked."

Olivia moved away from Neville's side. His musky cologne was not to her liking. She saw the gray in his hairline, the comb-marks in his hair. "Thank you, Neville. You think of everything." She had intended to send out the invitations herself, but Neville had the customer list. In the years she had been away she had lost touch with the town and with her father's clientele.

"I do my best, Miss Olivia." Neville turned to the center table and straightened the display of newly arrived cashmere sweaters. How many times had she heard her father explain to a customer, "Young Neville, here, will know your measurements. He keeps all our records." And indeed, Neville kept the leather-covered book meticulously filled with everyone's fabric choices and changes in weight, noting sagging muscles and expanding waistlines.

Jonas Willard sat in her father's office, in her father's leather chair and behind his oak desk. Olivia and Neville took the upright chairs facing him while he arranged his papers. Jonas Willard read her father's will without a preamble, and Olivia learned that the business, in its entirety, had been left to Neville. There was adequate monetary compensation for Olivia, but the wording of the will was undeniable. And why, she wondered, had Jonas allowed her father to write "dear" when mentioning Neville's name?

She watched Neville's face as the solicitor tucked the papers back into their dark folder. He had stolen the store from her. He was no longer "Young Neville." His hairline had receded; his cheeks were thinner. Neville was a middle-aged man who had snatched the Benton store from its rightful owner.

Jonas Willard coughed. He looked at Olivia and gave a little smile. "I'm sorry, my dear, but those were your father's wishes." He shook her hand and nodded to Neville before closing the door gently behind him.

"I'd like to call you Olivia now, if I may," Neville said. He stood in his Benton suit, in her father's store, and Olivia was surprised by the flood of emotion that swept over her—whether of embarrassment or rage, in that moment she couldn't decide. There was no way she could work in her father's store under Neville's proprietorial eye. She ignored his outstretched hand.

"Call me Miss Olivia, Neville. There has been no change in our relationship."

Olivia arrived at the hotel with a violent headache and shaking hands. She managed to pour a glass of red wine without spilling it and took a long drink.

Her clothes smelled of gasoline. She needed a shower and a more stylish outfit, one that would be suitable for the police, for the fire chief, for an appointment with Jonas Willard. As she showered, Olivia wondered what would be required now of her, the haberdasher's daughter, and whether Neville had made it down the narrow back stairs in time.

The Elephant

"Ginny," Harry said, arms spread to embrace me. I held his forearms and leaned into his kiss, a quick dab of moist lips on my cheek. The airport, late afternoon, was teeming with people. "Uncle," I said, "how was the trip?" I embraced my Aunt Lela while Harry hugged my daughter Sarah. On the way to the car, Lela, in heels and a shiny silk dress, kept up with Harry's long strides with small running footsteps, all the while thanking me for our hospitality.

"Thank you, thank you, so kind, Ginny."

Harry stacked the suitcases in the van, his suit still neat after the long hours in the plane, shoes carefully polished. His hair was gray now; his small moustache neatly trimmed over his upper lip, designer glasses in place. He had changed very little in the decades since he left for Thailand.

While Harry and Lela unpacked their bags, Sarah came into

the kitchen and leaned against the counter. She crossed her arms on her chest.

"I don't like him." My daughter, Sarah, was eight, petite, hair pulled back in a ponytail, rubber flip flops on her bare dusty feet.

"They're leaving tomorrow," I said. I was waiting for the phone to ring, for my mother to ask if her brother had arrived safely, if the plane had been on time, was he looking well?

"They're leaving tomorrow?" Sarah asked.

"For heaven's sake, Sarah, what's the problem?" My head was thick with supper preparations. I stirred the soup, my mother's hearty chicken and vegetable recipe.

"He smells," Sarah said. "I don't like him smoking cigars."

"Please set the table, Sarah." Outside the kitchen window the sun's warmth was cooling. "The blue napkins, the usual wine glasses."

Harry came through the kitchen. "Your garden has grown," he said. "Is there time for me to take Lela on a little tour? It's still light enough outside."

"Of course." And through the open window I heard Harry naming the flowers and shrubs that were foreign to his wife.

"Lovely, very lovely." Lela's voice was light and carrying.

Sarah hadn't moved. "He hugs me too close. I don't like it."

The knife I was using slipped on the baguette's crust. "Damnit, Sarah." I wrapped a paper towel around the cut on my finger. "Please get a Band-Aid."

"Mum!"

"Just get a Band-Aid," I repeated.

Those long hugs. I must have been about Sarah's age when Harry visited that last Christmas. I wanted to ask my mother why his hugs didn't seem right, why his breath smelled, but my mother was sad her brother was leaving, and she was in no mood to listen.

Lela came in from the garden. “Can I help?” Her nails were painted deep red to match her lipstick. She and Harry had no children and I wondered how she filled her days.

“Ah! You cut yourself.” She nudged me aside. “I will do it.” And as I warmed the baguette and made the salad dressing, Lela described her brothers and sisters, how she looked after their babies while they worked; how busy her days were with Harry traveling so often.

“Your husband? He travels much?” Lela put the lettuce into the serving bowl and blanched the asparagus.

I watched the precision of Lela’s movements, the delicate arranging of the food. The baguette slices formed a perfect circle on the plate, the small tomatoes became tiny flowers, the asparagus spears were rolled in the ham slices and nestled among the lettuce leaves.

“It’s his business. Like Harry, he travels a lot.”

“And you,” she said. “Only one child?”

Her question unsettled me. *Only one child*? Could she see by my face that our marriage was troubled?

“Ah,” Lela reached around my arm and wiped down the stove top. “I ask too many questions.” She rinsed out the dishrag and hung it neatly over the faucet. “Where is Sarah?”

My daughter was swinging in the hammock slung between the veranda uprights. One bare leg trailed over the edge of the hammock, her sandal slapping the floorboards. Uncle Harry sat on the wicker chair nearby. He had a cheroot in one hand and they might have been talking, but Sarah was gazing out into the garden and sucking on a strand of pale hair.

Lela touched my arm. “Your daughter looks much like you,” she said.

"Yes," I said. "Everyone says that."

Sarah swayed in the hammock.

My mother would be furious if I spoiled her brother's visit again, so for my mother's sake, I needed to be polite, and in the morning he would be gone.

"You well?" Lela's voice was filled with concern.

"A little tired," I said. "I need to call Sarah for supper."

She had been the same age as Sarah when Harry last visited. Her mother had found her on the verandah of their old house, swinging in a similar hammock and holding a little paper origami elephant. She was sucking on the ends of her hair, a habit her mother found irritating.

"Uncle had me sit on his lap."

"You're much too big for that," her mother had said. "Really, Ginny, what were you thinking?"

"He said I should have a ponytail." She couldn't tell her mother that when he gathered back her hair, he had held her too tightly.

"Don't be silly, Ginny," her mother had said. "Why do you always spoil things?" Later that evening when she swung in the hammock, watching the moths hit the light fixture, she heard her father and Harry arguing. They were in the garden, and their loud words, their angry insults, frightened her. She had felt anxious and guilty, and then relieved when Harry left the next day.

Lela was speaking to me. "I will ask for them to come, yes?"

I was holding the kitchen knife so tightly I thought my finger might bleed again from the pressure. "Thank you, yes," I said.

Lela tapped Harry on the shoulder and called to Sarah, and as Sarah scrambled out of the hammock, Lela caught her in her arms for a quick hug. They came into the dining room together, arm in arm. Harry stubbed out his cigar and followed.

The meal was pleasant, a family gathering. I gathered up the soup bowls and served the salad while Harry described his latest trip to Singapore, the cleanliness of the streets, the art, the food.

"I have a gift for you," Harry said to Sarah. "I'm sorry we're not staying longer. Business demands make this visit short."

"That's thoughtful of you, Harry." I nodded to Sarah to respond.

Sarah speared one of the perfectly formed tomato flowers. "Thank you, Uncle." Her knee was bouncing in that nervous habit she had.

Harry pulled a parcel from his pocket. Inside the box was a small jade elephant, its trunk raised over two tiny ivory tusks.

"It's to wish you good luck," Harry said with a smile.

"Trunk raised means happiness." Lela patted Sarah's arm. "Much happiness."

Sarah fingered the little elephant. "It's so fragile," she said. "Thank you Uncle Harry." She stood the gift by her plate and smiled up at her aunt.

Visitors bring gifts. Did Harry remember the little elephant he had given her many years ago? The origami elephant fashioned from brightly colored paper. "For good luck," he had said then. When she showed it to her mother she had smiled. "It's his thank-you gift." It was one of those moments when she needed a hug but her mother was not one to hug easily. She wanted to ask, *what happened?* but the words wouldn't come.

Lela passed the plate of salad to Uncle Harry who lifted the fresh green lettuce onto his plate beside the neat little rolls of ham.

"It's been a lovely visit," he said. "Such a long time since I was here last." He closed his eyes as he recalled the memory. "You remember, Ginny? That was the year I left for Thailand."

I pressed my hand against my knee. "You also gave me an elephant, a little origami elephant."

"A gift," he said. "You were a lovely child." He paused, fork in hand. "And now you're a lovely young woman." His face radiated goodwill as he glanced at my daughter, "Sarah looks very like you."

"What time are you leaving tomorrow, Harry?" I asked.

"We'll leave quite early," Harry lit his cigar. "It's a long drive."

"Mother will be so glad to see you."

After the meal, I stacked the dishes in the sink and watched the food scraps swirl in the water, tiny bits of detritus draining away. I felt Sarah come to my side. I wiped down the counter, placed the dishcloth neatly over the faucet, and wrapped my arms around my daughter in a long, long hug.

Sarah Wilcox

Sarah Wilcox fought the dust in her house as though it was an enemy sent by the devil himself. It was a provocation she could not ignore. Mornings, she wielded her broom over the kitchen floor and out to the back verandah, the length of the boards, from door to back wall, where a long cupboard held the bottles of fruit she had put up that summer. Every time she opened the cupboard door her heart swelled with pride until she saw how the dust reached onto those bottles and covered them.

The dust that swept in from the road made her itchy and restless. The wind came from west to east, down that dirt road, through the wire netting fence, drenching the back yard garden. Depending on the fierceness of the wind, it brought a veil of grayness to the bright leaves of her plants, covered her tomatoes and the runner beans climbing the wooden trellis. It dulled everything.

Summer and winter, it made no difference, the dust came. In the spring she dragged the floor rugs out, one by one, threw them over the outdoor line and beat them until her arms ached. They never felt clean. Grit and dust clung to the fibers, as though deliberately defying her efforts.

She understood her mission, her responsibility. It was a daily battle that lingered foremost in her mind.

She wore out words as she tried to explain to her husband why she was so agitated, why when the wind started in the trees she reached for the duster. Why she hung the mop and broom within easy reach.

Brian never understood. Working at his daily crossword, he murmured words of encouragement and sipped his green tea. He was proud of his wife; she was a comfort to him, providing regular hot meals and clean pajamas each Monday. He was proud of the way she kept the house, proud that she was frugal and spent within the allowance he gave her. He had heard stories about spendthrift wives who were never happy with what their husband provided, but his wife, his Sarah, was a true blessing.

Then, one bright summer morning, Sarah had a visitor. A blue van arrived in the front driveway and a man she didn't recognize came to the door. He was an ordinary looking young man in a dark blue suit and a wide smile.

He held his cap in his hands. "Are you the lady of the house?"

Sarah hurriedly untied her apron and took off her rubber gloves. She was glad she had cleared the breakfast dishes and swept the kitchen floor. She fluffed her hair slightly and looked the young man over.

"Who are you looking for?" She folded the gloves into her apron. "My husband's at work, if you want him, he'll be home at 5:00."

"I'm looking for the lady of the house and do I have a surprise for her!" The young man widened his smile and his whole body trembled as though he was enjoying a huge joke only he understood.

"A surprise?" Sarah straightened the belt at her waist.

"If you'll allow me?" He held out his hand. "Mrs. Wilcox? Please call me Herman."

And there was his hand, ready to be clasped. Sarah drew in a short breath and took his hand. "What is this about?"

"I am the Electrolux Man." He squeezed her hand ever so gently and pointed to his van in the driveway.

Sarah squinted against the sun. She saw some dusty lettering and read "Electrolux Vacuum Cleaners" in faded blue writing. Hadn't the Bowen sisters been talking about a salesman in the area? Hadn't one of them said that Jane Leask had bought a new machine from a salesman last week? That it was a miracle machine, and the Bowen sisters had said they couldn't wait to see it and what a gift it was for a woman keeping house these days.

The young man waited patiently as Sarah thought through the enormity of what might be revealed to her. "I can show you the machine if you'd like," he said. "I can provide a demonstration."

Would Brian approve if she allowed a salesman into the house? The young man looked quite clean; his suit was rumpled but that happens if you're in a car all day. His shoes were dusty, but she'd ask him to wipe them. If Jane Leask had admitted him surely it would be acceptable.

"Did Mrs. Leask ask for a demonstration?" Sarah had to be sure.

"Mrs. Leask?" he seemed to be thinking. "Why, yes, she did. On Patterson Drive?" He brought his hands together. "Yes, last week. She was very happy with my demonstration," he paused and repeated. "Very happy."

Those words settled her doubts. Traveling salesmen were rare in these parts, but he appeared young and harmless and obviously had made at least one sale to a respectable woman in town. Jane Leask organized the yearly Christmas Fete and knew every trick there was for taking stains out of table linens. She was known to be an impeccable housewife.

"You have a machine to show me?"

A smile lit up his face. "I'll just be a moment," he said. And he ran down the steps and opened the rear doors of the van. He pulled out a large box and hefted it into his arms.

Sarah opened the front door wider. She noticed the railings along the verandah had been visited by the starlings again. She would wash those down as soon as she saw the machine and the van had departed.

Herman carried the box inside and opened it up. He brought out a sleek gray cylinder with a hose attached. The electric cord coiled across the carpet and Herman plugged it into the electric outlet behind a small table. Sarah watched his movements and admired his deftness.

"When did you dust last?" he asked. He smiled at her and his voice was without judgment.

"Yesterday." Sarah knew her carpets were undeniably clean. Animals were not allowed in the house. Her husband's spaniel, Sammy, was long gone and hadn't been replaced. "I sweep on Tuesdays, dust on Wednesdays," she said with pride.

"Of course, Mrs. Wilcox. I can see what a fine housewife you are." Herman took out a smaller box and carefully pulled out an assortment of attachments which he lined up on the floor. "These," he said, "will provide for all your needs. Sofa, curtains, flooring, carpets." Herman savored each word, his eyes flicking around the room as he named the places that might hold dust.

She looked at the variety of silver accessories and wondered how she could use them. Sarah washed the curtains each month, but the sofa cushions? She felt like a guilty child with her fingers crossed behind her back.

Herman set the machine together, and holding the long silver wand in his right hand, stood poised before her. Sarah realized she was holding her breath.

"Are you ready, Mrs. Wilcox?"

Sarah nodded.

Time stood still as Sarah watched Herman move from one end of her large central rug to the other end, then from side to side. The machine stopped. Herman took out a large white handkerchief and placed it neatly on the floor. He took a bag out of the machine and emptied the contents. Sarah drew in a quick breath. The machine had sucked up a sizable amount of dust from her newly beaten rug.

Herman smiled. "May I go on?" he asked.

He set in a new attachment and vacuumed the floorboards in the dining room, moved smoothly into the kitchen, then circled back to the front door. The pile of dust and grit swelled on the white cloth.

"Would you like me to vacuum your drapes now?" Herman asked, eyeing the curtains hanging on the living room windows.

"No," Sarah said quickly. "That won't be necessary."

"Then let me show you the attachments," Herman said. He named each item and explained how easy the machine was to use, how little electricity was needed. Herman put all the vacuum parts neatly away while Sarah stood and stared at the pile of dust on the white handkerchief. Where had it come from, she wondered, after all her sweeping, her dusting?

"We have very good purchasing terms," Herman explained. "It can be yours, Mrs. Wilcox, with a small deposit, and monthly payments." He gathered up the white cloth, carefully folding the dust away from her gaze.

"When my husband comes home," she said. "We will discuss it." She looked at her curtains above the sofa and wondered what lay hidden in the folds.

"Here is my business card, Mrs. Wilcox. Do you have any questions?"

Sarah put his card on the little table and opened the front door. He passed by her with a brief smile and, "I do hope to hear from you soon, Mrs. Wilcox. Our supplies are limited."

"Will you be in the area for long?" she asked.

"I have an appointment with Miss Bowen," he said. "And then with Mrs. Howe."

Lizzie Howe? She volunteered at the post office on weekends. If Lizzie had one of these machines, she'd never hear the end of it. And if Lizzie could buy the machine, why couldn't she? Brian watched their household expenses with an eagle eye but he also liked a well-run house, a clean house, a dust-free home.

Sarah watched as Herman put the box in the back of the van, and she stood in the doorway as Herman drove out to the road and beyond.

All afternoon, Sarah was restless. She picked up her knitting and dropped it back into the basket after a few rows. She picked dead flowers off her houseplants and watered the petunias by the back door. She prepared the meatloaf for supper and as she was cutting up the onion she felt tears on her cheeks. She imagined that machine in her hands, imagined running that shiny nozzle over the rugs, under the sofa, across the floorboards, up the curtains. Her work would be so much easier. She would conquer the dust, the house would be clean. Sarah wiped her eyes on the corner of her apron.

Brian arrived home at 5:10 after a difficult day in the office. He was an accountant, and that afternoon some figures would not add up. He wanted a warm meal and the crossword in today's paper. Above all, he wanted a peaceful evening in his favorite chair.

Sarah had his meal ready to serve. She was anxious, fussing with her napkin, playing with the meatloaf on her plate until she finally said. "Brian, the most extraordinary thing happened today!"

"Yes dear?"

The Electrolux man came this morning."

"Who?"

Sarah explained the event in detail. The machine was a wonder. A beautiful machine that removed the dust and grime no one saw. It sucked up the grit that was wearing out their rugs, it was where the mites hid, the dust that caused their allergies. Herman's voice echoed in her head.

Brian shuffled his paper. He found his crossword and picked up his pen. Brian never used a pencil.

"That sounds nice, Sarah. Is there dessert?"

"Brian, I really want to have this machine. It would make the housework so much easier." She gathered the dishes off the table. "Could I have a little more allowance, dear? I could pay it off each month. Please, Brian, it would be quite wonderful."

Brian was not impressed. What would she do with the mops and brooms she already had? What a waste? He had believed Sarah was careful with her spending, then a salesman arrives, and immediately she wants this newfangled thing. He'd heard about salesmen and the way they seduced housewives into buying things they didn't need. And a vacuum cleaner? Who needs one of those? His mother never had one.

"Really, Sarah," Brian said. "You have everything necessary to keep the house clean." He marked in 2across. "You have an ample allowance." He wrote in 3down. "Surely you should be happy with that."

Sarah stood at the kitchen sink. She could see Lizzie Howe and Jane Leask both vacuuming their rugs, smiles on their faces, the mites and grit gathered in that little gray bag just waiting to be emptied. She sighed. All they needed to do was empty that little bag. She watched the dinner plates sink into the hot soapy water, and regardless of Brian's opinion, she decided she would have that machine.

Sarah spent a restless night.

On Monday evening Brian looked for his clean pajamas. Sarah always left them folded at the foot of the bed, and they weren't there. "Sarah," Brian called. "My pajamas?"

"I'm sorry, Brian. I was too busy cleaning the floors. I didn't have time to wash today." Sarah fluffed the cushions on the sofa and wondered how much dust they might hold.

"What do I do?" Brian's voice echoed down the stairs.

"Wear the one's from last night. I'll try and wash later this week." Sarah folded the granny-square rug neatly and settled it on the back of her chair. She was in no hurry to join Brian in bed. He would have to fold down the quilt himself and turn on the reading lights. They had their routines, and she was about to change them, a little prod here, a little prod there. She might mislay his paper tomorrow or overcook his lamb chop, instigate little irritations that would surely add up. She knew her Brian.

After a week, Brian was not sleeping well. He was irritable. He wondered what had happened to his ordered life, and more importantly, what had happened to his Sarah. She was not herself. She was tired, she left her mops and brooms out in the kitchen where he tripped on them. She left her dusters on the table and the dustpan in the living room. Some days she wasn't sure where she'd put his newspaper and when he found it under the cushions on his chair, it was crumpled.

On the following Monday evening when his clean pajamas were not folded on the end of their bed, Brian realized he needed to act. His Sarah was not happy. There was a message in her actions Brian was sure of that. He was a good provider, a kind man, he missed his Sammy but when it was time to put him down he understood. He thought hard about Sarah's happiness, and of course his, too, and he remembered her wish for that cleaning machine. Such a small solution in the grand scheme of things.

"Sarah," he called as he pulled on his pajama pants. "Sarah, that Electrolux man, what did you tell me about his machine?"

And Sarah smiled as she tidied the kitchen and switched on the dishwasher. "Lizzie Howe just bought the machine and her housework is done in a morning. Imagine that?" She went into their shared bathroom to clean her teeth.

Brian imagined his home life returning to normal. The washing of pajamas done on time. The mail and paper waiting on his chair. His evening meal ready, hot and nourishing. Brian stretched his aching back and climbed into bed.

Sarah turned down the quilt and climbed in beside him. "Having that machine is a perfect idea, Brian. Thank you, dear, I'll call Herman tomorrow, first thing." And she turned out the light.

White Tights and Spangles

I hadn't seen Martin Dougherty in a year, not since the last time I needed chairs. With a performing act like mine a woman needs strong chairs and when I arrived at *The Crow's Nest*, he came out from behind the counter with a welcoming smile on his face. "Good to see you again, Georgie." His two golden dogs padded out after him, sleek and brushed and friendly.

The shop smelled musty but Martin was fresh as a new pin. I gripped his hand. It was always good to see him. "You have some chairs for me, Martin?"

He gestured. "I got several," he said. "Beechwood, like you asked for." The two dogs settled near the shop doorway, heads on their paws.

We go way back, Martin and me, before his divorce from Denise, before I lost my Allen. We grew up on the same block, went to the same high school, dated twice, and then we were off to the city where our lives took different turns. It was years later that we met up again in the McFoy's Traveling Circus.

Back in the day he and Denise had a seven-dog act. Denise was the cheesecake, all dolled up, good legs, slim arms, and Martin did the work. She once confessed to me that she really didn't like the mutts. Their constant yapping gave her migraines and the dander made her allergies unbearable. It was not what she'd planned for her life so when Martin retired and bought the antique shop, she left. I'd guess dogs were only the tip of the iceberg.

I hefted one of the chairs. Beechwood chairs are best, strong and heavy. Nice color, too, though I've been known to paint my chairs for effect. Once I did a Fourth of July gig and painted them red, white and blue. It was an outside event and the audience loved it. I was slim then, white leotards catching the sun. On the first drum roll, I set one chair on top of the other, legs slotted for safety, three chairs in all. Another drum roll, I climbed that tower. Then the body swings up, and up. One hand on the back of the chair the other held out for balance, the crowd breaking into applause. Sometimes I put up a stool just for my own satisfaction, just to test myself, but I was never as brilliant as my Allen.

"New booking?" Martin scanned me with professional eyes. "You're looking fit, Georgie, sticking to salads these days?"

Was Martin flirting? It had been years since Denise left him.

"Business first, Martin," I said, a pat on his arm. "I do have a new gig." I checked the chairs he'd lined up for me. I held one of them in the air to test its balance. I go through two, maybe three chairs a year. Depends on how many bookings I have. It's an expense you need to plan for so I've found it's better to juggle plates and saucers most gigs, cheaper to replace.

I selected two chairs from the ones lining the wall.

"You paying cash?" Martin hustled the chairs into a pile and placed the two I'd selected by the door. "Nice thing about these, all being from the same set, Georgie, they're easy to stack."

I'm a gymnast and a juggler. Been doing it for forty years but I'm getting tired so now I do retirement homes. Word travels fast and I'm as busy as I want to be, though I shouldn't complain, it pays the rent, the broken chair legs, smashed china. It's a bit of a come-down from the best gigs I've had, like when we worked in McFoy's Circus. Allen and I trained with Eddie McFoy and his wife, learning acts that had passed down through generations. We were young and beautiful, ready for any challenge when the crowds were big and boisterous.

Martin had returned. He'd taken the chairs out to my truck and he was waiting to be paid. I don't use chairs as much anymore; juggling is a better act in retirement homes; cups and saucers on bamboo wands, multi-colored balls. It's fun when the oldies cheer, I pirouette, and on my best days, if there's space, I'll do a somersault. They love it. I'm a diversion in their regulated days. I'm party-time. Thank God they can't see well enough to notice the runs in my leotards or a dropped saucer or two.

Today was the eleven-year anniversary since Allen passed. A wave of nostalgia washed over me. Maybe it was the look Martin gave me when I first came into the shop when he noticed I'd slimmed down. A compliment is sometimes a signal, sometimes not, but there it was.

"Remember the Elks Club, Martin, that night a few years ago, the time iyou rescued me?"

Martin was placing coins in velvet-lined boxes. "That's where we met up again, Georgie. Could I forget?"

I sat on the bench by the door. "Remember what a rowdy mob they were, and I was a solo act with Allen gone. I'd done my juggling act, and I was balanced on three chairs, feet almost hitting the ceiling. I heard, 'Hey, Babe, great gams, great...' And that night you happened to be there, and you grabbed the fellow by his jacket and hustled him out of the hall."

Martin laughed. "What a ruckus that caused."

Martin was always the kind one. It was a cold night and I wasn't wearing much and he loaned me his coat.

Martin laughed. "Oh, Georgie, what a night it was." He burst into the old Elvis song, "*...oh what a night it was, oh such a night!*" and did a little two-step behind the counter. Martin had been a song and dance man once, light on his feet and a voice that could make you cry. Then he met Denise and they put together a performing dog act. Who would have guessed?

"You okay, doll?" Martin pulled a chair forward and sat down next to me. It was comforting to talk to someone who knew your life history: about the McFoys, about Allen and me, our lives together before the accident.

I put my face in my hands and caught my breath. Our act was headlined *Six Chairs to Heaven.* The circus had set up the day before and we'd all been glad of a good night's sleep. Everyone was out of their wagons enjoying the sun. Lines had been strung up, the washing was pegged out, and I'd hung our bedding to air after days of rain.

"You remember that night?" I asked Martin. My eyes began to burn. Eleven years since Allen died and every year I relived the event and the memory was still so vivid.

Martin nodded and rested his hand on one of the dogs.

It had been a wet April; the wooden chairs had swollen some, so we had difficulty getting the legs to hold in their allotted slots. I wore so many spangles I sparkled like a Christmas tree as I tossed the chairs up, one by one, six in all. As Allen positioned the last one, he moved from chair to chair, handstand to handstand.

He was like an automaton, each movement choreographed to best advantage. When the tableau was set, Allen swung himself up to the topmost chair. And the spotlight was full on his body, his white-slippered feet were pointing to heaven. People said he had iron biceps and we laughed at that, as if it was easy maintaining that strength.

"It happened in slow motion, didn't it Martin. I remembered how the top chair swayed and I watched Allen adjust his body a little to the left, then back to center. It was so quiet I heard gasps coming from the audience. "He was beautiful, wasn't he Marty?" I'd spent hours sewing those sequins on his costume and they were caught in the spotlight.

"He was," Martin said.

"Then he was falling." I gripped Martin's arm. "There wasn't a sound from the audience. It was slow, slow motion, like the world stopped spinning. And not a sound until he hit the boards. Not a bloody sound, until the chairs came crashing to the stage."

Martin put his arm around me. "It was a freak accident, Georgie."

"Oh, Marty, wasn't it awful?"

"I'll never forget," Martin said.

He was lying there in a circle of light until someone off-stage yelled to turn the goddam spotlight off. Two chairs were lying on top of Allen. His head was tipped at a terrible angle and there was blood. The ring master pulled me away and said how it looked bad, that I should get dressed.

Martin pulled me closer. "There, there Georgie, give it a rest."

"You never get over it, Marty, never. Every time I buy a chair it all comes back." His arm was still strong. Just because he had a dog act didn't mean he was weak or anything. The smell of his sweater was comforting, a little doggie, but what can you expect from a man who'd always loved dogs.

We sat together for a time.

"You know, Allen told me once he'd been bitten by a dog when he was a kid and that's why we never had a dog." The two golden retrievers stirred, waiting for their walk. "Allen had the teeth marks on his right buttock, a half-moon. I saw them the first time we got together."

"He was never easy with dogs," Martin said. "Your Allen and my Denise shared in that, neither knew a thing about animals."

I hadn't thought of Allen's dislike of dogs in a long time. How he'd back away when a dog tried to lick his hand, when one came to be patted.

"Come on, Georgie. Enough! I've got to walk the dogs down to the park." He reached for the leashes hanging by the door. "Let's close the shop and you and me take a walk. We can catch a beer at the pub on the corner."

Martin was asking me *out*. Maybe just to walk the dogs, but he was asking *me* out. After all this time we were going to walk out together. I wondered if he knew it was the anniversary of Allen's passing, that I felt unraveled, like when you're knitting and some stitches get dropped and there's a hole that you can't knit over. Life was really a balancing act. No matter what happened, you had to trust the show to go on.

"Marty," I said, standing and reaching for a leash. "What a lovely idea. The chairs can wait. Let me help you with the dogs."

And White Candles

Posey packed her workbook in her backpack. She and her older brother, Robert, were getting ready for school, same as always. Their mother stayed in bed since their father was gone, but her voice could be heard through the wall, calling. "Don't make a noise." And as they cleaned their teeth, "Hurry up. Don't miss the bus!"

Posey and her brother ate breakfast at the kitchen table, tipping out the cornflakes along with the dust in the cereal box. They ate in silence except for the *chomp, chomp* of her brother's jaws. The heat in the house had been turned off a week ago so they wore coats at the table. Their mother told them she only stayed in bed to keep warm, and they heard her coughing through the wall, coughing at night so much Posey buried her head in her pillow.

While Posey put the milk back in the fridge her brother left the room, and when he returned, he was holding her doll, Matilda, a gift on her ninth birthday.

"Here," Robert said. "You left it in the bathroom."

Matilda had black hair and delicate little fingernails. Sometimes her doll cried at night, so Posey pulled the blanket over both their heads, and they hugged each other tight. Matilda was wrapped in a striped blanket, a piece cut from the back of Posey's old winter dressing gown.

Posey knew she had to listen for the bus, but Robert was distracting her with the doll. Matilda's eye sockets were black holes. Last night her brother said he hated her doll, and he had grabbed the doll out of her hands and flipped it over and back, chanting, "Open and shut, open and shut," and then he had pushed Matilda's eyes into the back of her head so they couldn't open. His voice reminded her of the cat's wail when she stepped on its paw and Posey didn't know why Robert was being so mean, why everyone was so unhappy.

She reached out to take the doll. "Give her to me." Posey whispered the words knowing her mother was on the other side of the wall. Don't cry, she warned herself, just disappear. If she leaned against the white wall in the hall, she would disappear for the day, no school, no games, no teasing. She could stand against the wall among the shadows, right where the afternoon sun made patterns on the wallpaper dance and her brother would be alone.

But Matilda needed her.

Robert held the doll at arm's length and wagged it. He was grinning. The arms flopped. Posey wanted to hold Matilda before she disappeared into the wall. She took hold of one of the doll's arms and pulled gently. She thought her brother might let the doll go but instead, he grabbed the doll's legs and tugged Matilda out of her hands. Posey hated his teasing.

The hands on the kitchen clock reached the hour and chimed. The bus would be coming.

"You want her," Robert said. "Take her!" He threw the doll against the wall and she made such a clatter their mother called from the bedroom, "Haven't you gone yet?"

Her brother raced down the hall. Posey picked Matilda up and sat her in the stuffed chair and ran, her backpack thumping on her back.

"Come on!" It was the fat bus driver shouting. "Come on!" The motor was thrumming but he was smiling. Posey knew she'd find a seat up front where the odd kids sat. She hoped her mother wouldn't find her doll or throw it down the hall like she'd done in the past when she got angry. If she did, Matilda might land against the wall and hang there like a coat without a hook in her back. Posey could take her down later and Matilda would know she was safe. Even without eyes Matilda would know who rescued her.

"Come on already!" The driver called again. Posey scrambled into her seat.

The bus arrived at the school gates and Posey saw the big chimney behind the school send up dark smoke. She watched the smoke eddy into the blue shell of sky. If she flew up that old chimney on a pillow of smoke and disappeared, who would miss her?

The teacher was talking, tapping the blackboard with her wooden pointer.

Posey examined the wart on the end of her first finger, right where she held her pencil. The teacher said she held her pencil too tight. She had half-moons at the base of her nails and once her mother had painted her nails bright red. "There," she'd said. "Posey's ready for the Ball."

Posey didn't understand.

"A Ball, Posey, like a big dance where the girls wear pretty dresses and high heels." Her mother stroked her hand. "When you get big enough, you'll go to dances and if you're lucky you'll find someone to dance with."

"And will I marry him?" Posey asked.

Her mother dropped her hand and turned her head. "A word of advice, darling, there are no nice boys left in the world." The bedroom door slammed, and the living room darkened. Posey wondered about her mother's words. Robert was mean sometimes but other times he was kind like when he helped her with her schoolwork. And their father had read stories to them and made her laugh, but that all happened a long time ago.

This day at school was like all the other days. It was to be endured. It was busy, and the teacher was talking all the time while chairs screeched, and students moved. Posey's bathroom break was where the quiet happened. She never hurried. Whether she had to go or not, she sat, sometimes counting to a hundred before she flushed. She held her hands under the cool water, wiping and washing, wiping and washing, watching the water run. The water splashed in the bowl and the drops sprang and plopped against the dank metal.

And then the bus was there to take them home and the fat man was calling, "Hurry up, hurry up!"

When Posey got home, she put her school bag on the table and pulled out her math homework, rows of numbers to be added together. The light beside her father's empty chair made the ferns by the window grow into monstrous shapes. Posey hated those ferns. They made shadows on the wall where a framed picture, "The Wounded Stag" had hung. The picture had been dark and the arrows in its great humped shoulder brought on nightmares.

Their father had brought it home one night and hung it on the wall above the potted ferns. He said he'd won it.

And their mother said, "You been down with the clown show again?"

Posey didn't know what the clowns did at his work, but she saw her father holding balloons and her father somersaulting between desks. It looked like fun and maybe that's how he won things.

"You can't hang that in here!" their mother said. "Really. Steven, what the hell were you thinking?"

Her father said, "Look at that beast. Isn't it magnificent?" He straightened the frame against the wall. "What do you think, Robbie?"

"It's a bit gloomy, Dad, you know he's dying."

"Rubbish! Robbie. That stag owned the world. He was king out there."

"I hate it," their mother said. "Just get rid of it." Their father's face soured. He reluctantly took the picture down and put it out on the back porch.

"Take it out to the dump, Steven," their mother said. "Don't, for God's sake leave it there!"

Soon after the stag disappeared, their father packed his duffel bag and left home, and their mother locked herself in the big front bedroom.

"I have homework to do." Robert said to Posey as he came into the living room and sat down at the table. "Don't interrupt me."

Posey had finished her homework, so she picked up Matilda from the stuffed chair and shook her. She heard her doll's eyes rattle in her head. He shouldn't have done it. Posey knew where the bandages were kept in the bathroom cabinet so she retrieved one and carefully wrapped it around Matilda's head, closing off the two empty eye sockets. She pinned the bandage in place. Matilda looked like she'd returned from a war and Posey was the nurse. She cradled the doll in her arms and in her head, she sang a lullaby. Matilda was sleeping.

Their mother appeared. She wore her old dressing gown, the one with ridges, the one that smelled. No one had been washing any clothes lately. Posey didn't know how to use the machine, but she knew her bedclothes should be washed soon. And her clothes. Even her brother smelled like stale potatoes when the eyes began to grow strings.

"I'll make supper," their mother said. "Has anyone done the shopping?"

Robert looked up blankly. "How do we pay for it?"

"There's money in the tin." Their mother went into the kitchen. "He left some money on the table. It's in the red tin."

Posey heard her mother moving things around. She dropped something heavy, and it rolled along the floor. "Someone come and pick the honey up," she called. "Can't you see I'm busy?"

Their mother came back into the living room, and her brother looked up. "Are you going to buy some food?" he asked.

"Don't rush me. I'll put on some clothes. McDonald's will do tonight." She held the door frame. "I'll get groceries tomorrow."

"I'm starving," Robert said. He bent over his book and went on working.

Posey held her wounded doll. "Can I come with you?" Posey asked. Her mother swayed as she held the door frame. "Another time." She walked unsteadily to the bedroom and shut the door.

Posey waited. She heard shuffling but her mother didn't come out.

After a while her brother looked up from his books. "Get the money, Sis," he said. "I'm calling Aunt Bea now."

Posey lifted the red tin down from the shelf where the tall bottles were kept: soy, ketchup, olive oil, vinegar, nothing there to eat. The tin had once contained chocolate powder and was dark red with pretty twirly designs around the edges. Inside the tin were dollar bills.

"How many do I need?

Robert sighed. "Twelve, I guess." He turned the page of his book. "How many are left?"

Posey counted out twelve and put the other bills back in the tin. She replaced the lid. "Five left."

"It'll be alright. I'll call Aunt Bea." Aunt Bea was their mother's sister. Posey remembered sitting on her aunt's soft lap and when Aunt Bea hugged her it felt like being squeezed between two soft pillows.

"You'll have to go." Robert slapped his workbook closed. "Don't argue, Posey. We've got to eat tonight. And I have to finish this homework."

"It's dark out there, Robbie, Matilda won't like it."

"I've got to watch Mom." He held the telephone to his ear, and she heard the ringing. "You know where McDonalds is? Get three hamburgers and be quick." Robert stared at her. "You need a coat, okay?"

Posey put on her yellow raincoat and knitted hat. She put the money in her pocket. "Will Aunt Bea come?"

"Maybe tonight, maybe tomorrow. She'll know what to do." Her brother's face looked white like the paper in his book. "Take Matilda with you."

"I don't want to go." Posey stood at the open door. The wind was brisk, and her raincoat wasn't very warm. She tucked Matilda inside her coat, against her chest. She'd grown this past year, so her raincoat was snug around her body.

"You can do it," her brother called.

Streetlights lit the pavement. There was no one out now, everyone was eating supper. Posey imagined candles and silver forks and food on china plates. One day she was going to have lots of candles, big, fat white candles like she'd seen in church one time. She patted the front of her raincoat and knew Matilda was warm inside.

The McDonald's arch at the end of the block showed golden against the night sky. The place smelled of hot oil and coffee. A poster on the back wall showed a birthday party with balloons and streamers and children in their best clothes, and there were buckets of McDonald's food on the table beside the birthday cake. Posey leaned against the counter, her eyes on level with the top.

"Yes, love, what you want?" Posey knew the woman. She worked in the lunch kitchen at the school doling out hot dogs and oranges.

"Three hamburgers, please."

"You want three fries, too?"

"Yes, ma'am."

The woman wrapped the burgers and shoveled out a cup of fries. She put everything in a paper bag covered with golden arches. "You got the money?"

"Yes."

"Count it out, love." Posey handed over her twelve dollars. The notes felt sticky and damp.

"That's not enough." The woman put her hands on her hips. "I've seen you at school, right? You've got an older brother."

"He's starving and mom's not well." Posey felt cold inside her raincoat.

The woman behind the counter looked at her. "You okay?"

she asked. Two men came through the door and stood behind her. They were big, laughing men and they were so close she felt their warmth.

The woman handed over the paper bag. "Just this once," she said. "Not again, you hear?"

The paper bag was warm in Posey's hands. "Thank you, ma'am." She ran to the door. The street was darker now. She had seen a picture in a magazine of a table at Thanksgiving with a family sitting around. There was a white tablecloth and the biggest, brownest turkey on the table surrounded by big plates of vegetables, too many to name. She thought she remembered lots of tall white candles on that table, too, and the light from the candles was golden.

Posey sat on the seat outside the dry cleaners and held the warm paper bag. She unwrapped the bun, smelled the melted cheese, and took a bite. She'd tell her brother she only had enough money for two burgers and fries. She looked in the bag. She wiped her mouth with the paper napkin and took out a handful of fries. They could split the remaining burgers and fries three-ways. Her brother was good at doing that, dividing up food.

She folded the top of the bag over twice to keep the warmth inside. She thought she saw her mother walking down the street toward her, her dark coat flipping up in the wind. But it couldn't be her mother, this person was larger and rounder and when the streetlight lit her face she knew it was not her mother.

"Aunt Bea!" Posey ran to her. "You came! You came!"

"Robert told me where you were. Such a big girl to come out on a night like this and all on your own." She hugged Posey and Matilda slipped from beneath Posey's coat and fell to the ground.

"Is that Matilda?"

"Robbie said to bring her so I wouldn't be scared." Posey

picked Matilda up and straightened the bandage on her head. "Her eyes have gone. She can't see anymore."

"Poor Matilda," Aunt Bea said. "We'll have to fix her then, won't we?"

Aunt Bea walked Posey back to the seat. "We'll sit for a moment, and you can tell me what you have in the bag?"

"I ate some already."

"McDonald's, is it?" Aunt Bea put her arm around Posey's shoulder. "We'll need more than what's in the bag if we're going to sleep tonight."

Posey felt the power of her aunt. Her big black coat was warm. Her woolly red scarf matched her woolly red hat. "The house is cold and Robbie's starving." Posey stopped to catch her breath. Aunt Bea had come to save them. From the comfort of that warm arm, Posey whispered, "It's going to be alright now, isn't it Aunt Bea?" She would take care of Matilda's eyes and make their mother better. She would turn on the heat. Maybe she would find some white candles, too, for the kitchen table, when they all ate supper together.

The Lost Dear

Shelley saw them. She left her car in the driveway and rushed up to the house, *knocking, knocking,* and when I opened the door, she was a little breathless, "There are three deer by the garden shed!" Her city eyes were wide with her discovery.

"Three deer," I said. "Are you sure?"

She laughed as I wheeled her suitcase along the hallway to the guest room. "They were just like big dogs," she said. "And their coats," she stopped for a moment in the doorway, "their coats were like hot caramel."

I hadn't seen any deer since I'd picked up my husband's red cap from the hard ground one year ago. It was early spring down by the lower garden where the deer gathered under the broad branches of the hemlocks, where they birthed their small wobbly-legged offspring. Those fragile creatures delighted me, and why, I always wondered, were there twins?

"We'll have green tea on the patio," I called to my friend and left her to unpack. Half a century earlier, Shelley had been my roommate at college and then my only bridesmaid. Nothing had disturbed our friendship in all those years and here she was, ready to spend some time with me, city to country, busy streets to a stony back road.

"I love this soap," Shelley called from the guest bathroom. "Where did you find it?"

I went back to the window and parted the curtains. If Shelley had seen the deer surely they'd still be there beside the shed. My husband, not a carpenter but using a how-to book, had proudly built the shed and stained it dark red. It had taken all one summer, sawing and sanding, settling the ladder on uneven ground. I was afraid he might lose his balance while hammering the roofing tiles, that he would fall, that he could break bones.

From the window I searched the back ledge where the ferns grew in abundance.

Last year three deer had camped out on the dense pile of leaves we'd left beneath the hemlocks. I suspected a doe and her twins. I had watched them while my husband hauled a load of grass clippings to the compost bin. Then I heard him cry out. He had been dragging the blue tarp down the bank and over the daylilies when he fell. I saw his red cap drop behind the still bare branches of the forsythia. One moment his cap was visible, clearly defined against the green of the upper bank, then it was gone. I watched as the tarp billowed out, caught in the sudden updraft of air, the old tarp he'd used while painting the shed, still with red paint along one ragged end.

"Why not buy a new one," I had suggested when he was painting the shed. He had lined up the brushes to dry and was scrubbing his hands. "We can always use two tarps," I said.

"Then, why not three," he replied, "one for painting, one for the leaves." He'd paused, hands in the air like a surgeon readying for an operation. "And one more tarp just in case it's needed." Then, enjoying his joke, he laughed.

"Three tarps then." I added it to my grocery list. We didn't spend on things we didn't need so I wondered about buying a third tarp. My husband was always so careful with money, so well organized, but last year he had also ordered two hundred daffodil bulbs. Two hundred seemed an exorbitant number, but he thought a sea of yellow heads would be worth the effort even though he was unsure the bulbs would survive.

"Not likely to happen," our neighbor on the south side of our property had said as we were setting the bulbs. "Too dry," he concluded. "Waste of money." We went ahead anyway and planted the bulbs. They bloomed lavishly and our pessimistic neighbor left a bottle of wine on our doorstep with a note of congratulations. We never needed the third tarp and it remained in the garage still in its clean plastic wrap.

"Are they still there?" It was Shelley calling from the guest room.

There were no deer beside the shed that I could see. My husband had built the shed using discarded boarding and secondhand windows, discarded tiles and someone's abandoned front door. The afternoon light played over the boards where, this year, some of the red stain had bleached out in the sun. The square of glass in the wooden door reflected the light oddly. Old glass does that, shifting and splitting the rays.

I didn't know Shelley was in the room until she touched my arm. "They were grazing," she said. "They do graze, don't they?"

"I'm not sure," I said. "I can't remember anymore." I dropped the curtain and wondered at the small water stain along its hem.

"We didn't have time to rake the leaves last year so there's nowhere for the deer to rest." I wondered if that was true or whether I was skirting the momentous moment of change when only the flapping blue tarp had occupied my mind.

Shelley put her arm around my shoulders. "They'll come back," she said. "Now tell me where you found that lovely soap."

I leaned into my friend. My husband's red hat hangs on a peg in the closet downstairs and when the temperature drops outside, I pull it on. I wore it this winter when I was gardening because it was big enough to cover my ears. And it was his ears that first caught my attention. He could wiggle them. A mutual friend introduced us. "This is our resident Hobbit," she'd said. He had opened his eyes wide and wiggled his ears. We found we'd both read Tolkien's trilogy. Then he asked me out.

We were engaged when we found the house we both loved. We stood on the hill, looking out over the fields below while the September winds had swirled up to where we were standing, and I had suggested he buy a hat to cover his ears.

"Something red," I suggested. "So I can see you from the house."

"Rubbish!" he'd said. "My ears are impervious to cold." But he bought the red knitted cap and because of his rather large ears he wondered about having children. "They'd all look like Hobbits." He'd laughed deep in his belly and his eyes closed. I loved his ears. They gave him a comical expression, an endearing goofiness. It was only later, after we were married, that I learned he had been serious about not having children.

We were digging the first perennial garden by the house when he told me he'd seen a doctor and had the procedure.

"This earth won't support any more children," he said reasonably, turning his wedding ring to dislodge the dirt caught against his knuckle.

"But why didn't you talk to me? There are two of us involved in this decision." I had wanted children and I felt my eyes water suddenly. I'd planned for two, three at best, in my mind always a large noisy family. My sister had twin boys. My brother had five girls. I was breathless in the face of his composure.

"With global warming," he said and made an expansive gesture that included the hill of hemlocks and the sky above. "I thought we were in agreement on that, the climate problems ahead." Before we were married we had long discussions about climate change, how there wouldn't be enough food for everyone, how the migration of people would impact us all. I believed, but I didn't know how deeply he believed and it had nothing to do with his ears.

"Some things can't be reversed, can they?" I finally asked him.

Of course we argued. I thought of ending our marriage. The loss settled in my chest, a tight knot, until I thought I was having a heart attack. I went to New Mexico for three months. It was lonely, being one person, hiking the windswept hills. I returned and he hugged me so tightly I thought, how can it matter? We knew many couples without children and soon after we joined a wine tasting club.

We didn't discuss babies anymore. I mourned in silence and dug more flower gardens. He bought more and better tools for his tool shed while I ordered garden catalogues and dug vegetable beds. We planted spring bulbs and I knitted creamy-white layettes for my friends' babies. We built stone walls together on the north side and raised worms in our compost bins that we gave to our neighbors' children for their fishing adventures.

One day a pregnant neighbor met me in the street. "Here," she said. "Feel this." I held a bag of fruit in one hand so she placed my free hand on her belly. "Can you feel him kick?" she asked.

I steadied myself against the wall. "How wonderful," I said.

My friend laughed. "Aren't we lucky?"

"Indeed," I said. "That's one strong baby!"

I went home, had a hot shower and made a perfect quiche. I prepared a salad from the garden and opened a fine white Chablis. The living room was tidy, a flourishing white cyclamen posed on the glass topped table. Our three apple trees and lone pear tree produced beautiful fruit and our summer vegetables were admired by the neighbors, why ask for more?

Aren't we lucky echoed in my head, *lucky, lucky*, and then he burst through the door and in his hug I wondered how some things can't be changed.

Today, my friend Shelley had seen three deer, perhaps a doe and her twins. Three is a family. We were only two for fifty-four years. The longing never goes away.

After I had picked up his red cap and brushed it off there was just me. Just one. He fell and was gone. I had rolled up the old blue tarp and I remember how it turned and twisted in my hands, how it wouldn't conform, how I struggled. I stuffed it among the boxes in the garage along with the other two tarps, the one red stained and the third one unused, waiting for the "later times" that never came.

Shelley drew me away from the window. "The deer will return," she said.

We went to the patio and I poured the tea. After this past bitter winter some warmth was returning in the air. The last of the snow had left the vegetable gardens. The daffodils we planted will be blooming all up and down the slope, a blanket of yellow. The deer will return and Shelley will stay with me through these warmer months. There will be two in the house again.

Property Lines

I was visiting my sister in Maine when my neighbors put in their new driveway, a macadam driveway, as shiny black as my new patent leather shoes. From my bedroom window I could see that their new letterbox at the foot of their driveway was at least five feet over my property line. Five feet doesn't sound like much, but with property taxes so high in our county I was not going to pay for any part of this new work.

My neighbor was mowing the narrow strip of lawn alongside his driveway so I picked up my walking stick and made my way down through my garden, past the crabapple trees and flowering lilacs, until I reached their driveway.

"Hello," I called over the noise of his lawnmower.

They had moved in this past winter and I knew their surnames and that they worked at the local college, but little else. We tend to hibernate in New Hampshire's winter months and being of a certain age I rarely went out.

"Hello! Mr. Christis!" I raised my voice and by now I was in his sight. His driveway seemed steeper than I remembered when my dear friend, Laura Watkins lived here. This past year she had sold up and moved into a nearby nursing home.

"Mrs. Hobbes, is it?" Mr. Christis looked surprised and switched off the machine. "You have been away?" He was sweating so his T-shirt clung in wet patches to his brown skin. As I got closer, I saw he was younger than I expected.

"Mr. Christis, your driveway!" I called. "It's on my property."

"Are you all right, Mrs. Hobbes?"

"The driveway!" I raised my voice. "Can't you see the marker!" I pointed down the driveway with my walking stick at the small concrete marker.

"The marker, Mrs. Hobbes?"

At this moment their front door opened. "Mrs. Hobbes!" His wife must have heard the lawn mower stop. "I wanted to tell you, Mrs. Hobbes," she called as she walked down the steps. "Your crabapple trees are beautiful."

My husband planted those trees forty years ago. He'd placed a wrought iron bench under the largest tree for when I picked up the newspaper and needed a place to read in the morning sun.

"Lovely gardens," they chorused. Mr. Christis put his arm around his wife's shoulder and together we looked through the dividing hedge and into my property.

They appeared to be nice people, my neighbors, though they spoke English with a faint accent.

"Althea and I think your property is lovely," Mr. Christis said.

I looked at my trim hedges. There were years of work and planning in all that neatness. I was slower these days, an hour on this, an hour on that, and with my husband gone, I had a gardener do all the heavy work.

Mrs. Christis was speaking. "If you have any cuttings, anything you might be throwing away, Mrs. Hobbes, we'd be glad to have them."

Her husband chimed in. "We're thinking to start a garden, too."

I pushed a small stone off the path with my boot. What were they thinking? In New England the summers were short, growth happened slowly. When I divided plants, there was always a place on my property to put them. Their lawn was just coming in with many bald patches, and I knew their backyard was narrow, set between the house and a steep granite bank. The Watkins never tried to garden on this property so where would these new people put a garden?

"Well!" I tapped the driveway with my stick.

"No, no. I'm not asking for handouts," Mrs. Christis said. They seemed to move closer together then, hip to hip, his arm was pulling her in. "We love your gardens," she said again. "We can see them from our window."

I looked to where their living room windows overlooked my gardens and then down the driveway to their letterbox. I considered the distance between the concrete marker and the edge of the driveway. Five feet. The distance hadn't changed during our conversation, and this year's property tax bill had gone up again.

The neighbors were watching me. Her name was Althea, but I didn't know his Christian name, or whether they were Christians. I was surprised at the thought. Once we all knew each other on the street. We had pot-luck suppers together and exchanged recipes, and our children sang Christmas carols in the stone church. The street was always busy with strollers and small children, bikes and dogs.

I tapped my stick against my shoe. I was there because of those five feet of encroachment. "What will you do about this driveway?" I asked. "It's wrong."

"I don't understand. The driveway was surveyed. The work is done." They looked at me, two pairs of brown eyes. They were no longer smiling. Mrs. Christis placed her hands on her hips. "We spoke to you before you went on holiday."

My holiday. I still had to unpack my suitcase and drive to the grocery store, yet here I was, standing in my neighbors' front yard talking about letterboxes. I didn't know if they had children, or where their relatives lived, or how they found this house on my street.

No matter, their letterbox was on my property. When my husband was alive, he would have known what to ask, what to do, what papers needed signing. Every year he took our tax bill done to the Town Offices and registered a complaint. One year he had Bernie Dorr with him, our lawyer, and made a right old fuss.

"We had permission," Mr. Christis said. "By the town."

I'd heard stories on the local news about foreigners coming in without papers, taking jobs from local people. They didn't live by the same principles or know our laws, and some were born troublemakers. Of course, one couldn't believe all the stories one heard but where there's smoke there's sometimes fire.

"How long have you been in this country?" I asked, looking into his face.

"I was born here, Mrs. Hobbes. In the next state, across the river." Mr. Christis wiped his hands down his jeans. "My parents still live there."

"And your wife?" I didn't look at Mrs. Christis.

"Our families emigrated a generation ago."

I felt a little faint at this news, a little wobbly, my walking stick hit the ground, and then my knees hurt as they hit the new macadam. They might look like foreigners but they were Americans, second generation Americans.

"Mrs. Hobbes?" The neighbors were leaning over me, concern on their faces. "Are you alright, Mrs. Hobbes?"

"The property line," I whispered. "Can't you see the property line?" From my position on the ground, the new black letter box was definitely on my property.

They helped me to my feet, and Mrs. Christis picked up my walking stick. It was one of my husband's last gifts. If only he was here now he would have taken charge of the situation.

"You must come inside." Mrs. Christis held my arm. I was standing but a little shaky. She looked concerned. Her husband, and I couldn't recall if I'd heard his Christian name, looked unhappy.

"No," I said. "I must be getting home."

"Are you sure?" she hesitated. "My husband will walk you there."

"I'm quite alright, thank you." I straightened my shoulders and looked at their brown faces. They didn't look like anyone on the street that I remembered. In the last few years moving vans had come and gone, and when the older families left the road, younger families had bought their houses. I was the last of that generation to remain in my house, and I missed my old friends.

They walked beside me down the new driveway and we slowed by the new letterbox. I tapped it with my walking stick. "That's on my property," I said. "That's why I'm here."

"One moment, Mrs. Hobbes." Mr. Christis walked a few feet away from me. He kicked away some matted grass and leaves to uncover a gray concrete marker, and I saw that the letterbox was well within the property line. Then he approached the rounded stone I had mistakenly thought was the concrete marker and placed his boot on it.

Together we stared at the stone in silence.

"Anyone can make a mistake," he said. "Right, Mrs. Hobbes?"

"We have to keep the grass down," Mrs. Christis said quickly as she came to stand beside her husband. "The marker must be clear for the assessors to see."

Assessors? I understood her kindness. Perhaps they would become good neighbors after all. "I have some hardy Cranesbill geraniums." I glanced back up the driveway. This was no longer my friend's house. This young couple were now owners of my friend's house. "These hardy blue geraniums should do well here."

Mrs. Christis stood with her hand shading her eyes and I noticed her apron was printed with black and white cows. The quintessential Vermont milker.

"That's that then," I said. "Have a good day." And as I walked away, I remembered, I still did not know his Christian name.

Tasting Sweet Plums

My father stood on the far side of the lantana hedge gazing off at the sun's hazy glow on the three tall plum trees at the back of the house. His arms were tucked close to his body, and I heard the hard jet of water hit the ground.

We lived far out in the country and sometimes the privy down by the end of the yard, behind the trellis of flowering vines, was too much of a nuisance to make for. There was privacy beneath that great arch of sky that allowed us to do some things—open and upfront. I envied his stance, legs apart, set booted in the grass, and he stood straight up, straight tall to where his bushman's hat set back on his forehead. But it was the hard downward stream spilling its heat on the morning ground that fascinated me.

He must have heard me, for without turning his head, he called softly, "Carrie, go inside," and I waited as the last few drops of moisture fell before I turned to run back to the house. Later, I tried to imitate his style, so I was younger than I recall, and I hated it: the wetness dribbling down my bare legs.

Not long after this, I went to my parents' bed in the first light when they struggled from sleep and crawled in beside my mother. I knew it was a special treat, this permission to join my parents in their bed with its many pillows and mountainous eiderdown. I lay quietly in my mother's company, savoring the intimacy and the faint movements of the bedclothes as one of my parents settled into a new position, arranging an arm or a leg.

I brought my games into my parents' bed. I had grown to enjoy the solitary games I played with my imaginary friends who were more ready to do my bidding than Sue or Mary or Elizabeth Weir, more obedient to my flights of fantasy. They were marvelous games, and I played the hero in a million scenarios. With two brothers in the house who were older, wiser and stronger, I naturally became the hero of my dreams. Their books were more exciting, more dangerous, with families stranded on remote islands, adventures in Amazon jungles, pirates and buried treasure, while my books described good girls doing good things in safe situations.

But then my restless limbs and active little body became an irritation to my mother, who took a while to wake up, liked to come from sleep her way. So, one morning she said, or perhaps he said, I could be on his side of the bed for my fidgeting wouldn't disturb him, and for several mornings I lay quietly, my back turned to my father and my hands curled over the edge of the mattress into the cool recess where the sheet tucked under.

My father's body was hard: there were bones and sinews I never expected when I lay beside my mother where everything was velvety smooth. Her sweat had a flowery smell. His was different. His sweat smelled of peaches and plums when they're ripe and their scent comes in a lingering way before you snap one from the branch, take the first deep bite, and the juice runs over your lips.

He slept on two pillows which seemed a mark of honor, two fat pillows, and his head made a deep valley in the cradle of their plump whiteness. We all slept between white sheets and put our heads on rough white pillowcases. That's why Mondays were so busy for my mother. That was her wash day. The copper sat in the small shed at the back of the house and the wash was boiled in that great deep copper cauldron set over a brick fireplace where blocks of wood were laid and fired. The tubs were set beside the copper, two of them, and I'd heard her tell my father how good it was to have two: one for rinsing, one for blueing. Her whites just had to be white.

She used a long pole to lift and stir the clothes in the hot suds, steam making the material balloon above the surface of the soap bubbles. I liked watching her, her strength, the flush on her face as she flipped the clothes from the copper to tub—she had a delicacy of wrist movement that proved she knew what she handled. It was the only time her hair came loose and formed damp ringlets around her face, the only time I noticed her sleeves rolled to her elbows in quite that way. I never saw her arms quite so naked as on washdays.

I helped carry the basket of heavy wet clothes out to the clothesline beyond the vine-covered trellis, and she fastened each piece to the line as I handed up the wooden pegs. If the wind was blowing from the west the wet clothes blew into our faces and pulled at our hair. On days when we finished the loads early, she would make tomato and cucumber sandwiches for lunch and we would sit together with a pot of green tea.

My father's pajamas were cotton ones, striped blues and browns, with a neat pocket over his left breast that he never used. My nighties didn't have a pocket, but the green dressing gown my mother knitted for me had two pockets and my mother had a rule that we should never appear, after our baths, without dressing gowns over our night attire.

One summer evening when the rooms in the house were stifling from the day's heat and it was too hot to wear a dressing gown, my father took me outside to find the cicadas. It was in these twilight hours when he'd finished farm work that he taught me the names of the grasses, the birds, the proper names of all the oak trees, the names of the clouds that swept the sky. It was that time of day when the brothers were doing homework and mother was preparing dinner that we spent time together.

He took my hand this evening when the furry-bodied bomber moths circled the lantana blossom. The heat rose off the ground like a shimmering wall, as though we were seeing through a fine sheet of water, and the cicadas' chirruping in the cedar trees was deafening. His hand was large and rough around mine and I felt the scab of a recent work wound. He found an emerald-green cicada and placed it in my palm, its eyes were gently shaped. He placed a large black cicada alongside it and the black one was bold with spots of rusty orange on its glistening body. The chirruping sounds ceased as their wings rubbed against each other like dry leaves and the black one rose up, clinging with its tiny claws, to mount the green one. I formed a cup with my hands, enclosing them, and as I stood beside my father they burst into song.

He moved over in the bed and my mother murmured about the early hour of my coming. I saw a seam on the shoulder of his pajama top had opened and a tuft of hair had escaped. My father was a hairy man; thick fair curly hair covered his arms and legs and made us laugh whenever we enticed him to swim with us in the bottom dam. But there was no hair around the long-jagged scar that ran down his right leg, below the knee. He'd been cutting wood, his foot had slipped, and the axe cut his leg through to the bone in a great glancing blow that caused the blood to flow freely.

Mother was clever with a needle. She threaded some strong black cotton, and she stitched those flaps of skin together like the men sewed up bags of peas on my grandfather Phillip's farm, and as she sewed, she mopped up the red flow on her white towels and crisply ordered me to fetch a brandy, a stiff one. I remember the steady look that passed between them, no words were spoken; she worked against the pump of blood and my father's faintness. She kept a phial of morphine in the cupboard for just these occasions and later my father slept alone in their bed. I could never look at that scar, was always a little afraid of the puckered skin and the dark redness where it had healed poorly.

There, beside my father, I was aware of his hip and the solid depth of his chest. He lay with his two arms above his head, half-asleep, and as firm as the center post in a big farm shed. I placed my head on his chest and heard the beating of his heart, the breath rushing up through his body. My hand touched the hard round buttons of his pajama coat and the cord that tied his pants at the waist. It took only a moment to bring my hand to his hair, the dark wiry hair that sprang through the fly of his pants, and a further moment for my fingers to brush him, a light blind touch that brought a sense of a purple plum bursting its skin.

I listened to their even breathing and watched the eiderdown rise and fall, until my father's body jack-knifed to a sitting position. My mother asked what was happening as my father's feet hit the floor. I don't remember if I was carried back to my bed, if anyone tucked me in, what more was said, but I knew with a child's certainty that I was never to visit my parents' bed again.

The following summer, I gathered the fallen plums under the Santa Rosa tree, and as I dragged the bucket into the long grass at the tree's base, the heady fragrance of over-ripe fruit and damp earth was intoxicating. The plums were easy to find. I parted the thick grass, placing the firm ones in the bucket and discarding those which were rotten until I found the largest, most perfectly formed plum with a tang of wine-ripeness. It felt good in my hand. That plum I ate.

Over the Back Fence

Ruth brushed the bird droppings off the small outdoor table with a paper napkin and put down the tea tray. The table was shaded by a cedar tree where the local sparrows held their daily gatherings, and it was quite peaceful until she heard her neighbor digging on the other side of the fence. Roger Crow was scrambling among the oleander shrubs and their flowery heads were waving wildly above the top of the fence.

He was always digging. If Ruth stood on tiptoe and looked over the fence, she could see beyond the oleanders and rose bushes to the back of the house with its small patio and a table set under a dark blue umbrella. There were vegetable gardens and a trellis covered in jasmine, and some afternoons if the breeze came from the east she could smell the blossoms.

"Morning Roger," she called, loud enough to be heard over the shoveling. "What are you planting this season?"

"Kitchen compost," he called abruptly. "Good for the soil!" It seemed an awful lot of digging for a can of compost.

Roger was not one to engage in friendly chitchat and Ruth realized she was disappointed in her neighbors. She had heard their voices one evening as she swept the patio of dry leaves, his was raised and angry, hers was muffled. She had heard the slam of doors, and seen the light snap on in their upstairs bedroom. They were not the outgoing comfortable couple she had hoped they'd be.

Soon after she bought the house she had invited them to lunch, but they had declined. They liked their quiet ways, Didi Crow had explained, their routines, but Didi's head still floated above the back fence at least once a week to ask if Ruth was settling in, and if her baskets of fuchsia were attracting the hummingbirds. Didi was a slight woman with tightly curled hair and dark eyebrows, and a high-pitched, querulous voice. And that thought reminded Ruth she hadn't seen Didi for a week or more. She hadn't heard her voice either.

The Crows had a cat that visited her. Ruth had named him Thomas, not an interesting choice, but easy to remember. Soon after she moved into the house, she had been eating a ham and cheese sandwich at this same table and had dropped some of the filling, and Thomas came running through the hole in the fence. He ate the shred of cheese and left the little piece of ham. He loved cheese.

On Tuesday, while Ruth was eating her lunch and Thomas was sunning himself on the warm bricks, Roger Crow called to her.

"You there Ruth? My old tom over there?"

"He's here, Roger. He's joined me for lunch." Thomas sat up and licked his fur. He appeared to have no interest in returning to his owner even though Ruth knew he recognized his master's voice.

"He spends too much time over there. Come on, Brady, come on home."

Thomas continued to preen. Roger Crow's hat bobbed above the top of the fence. Brady? Ruth wiped her fingers. What a foolish name, she thought, until she saw the logo on Roger's hat. He was a Patriots fan.

"And how is Didi?" she called. "I haven't seen her in days."

There was no answer from behind the fence, but the digging stopped. She was going to get up and move closer to the fence when Roger Crow spoke. "She's off visiting her sister. In Boston."

"I hope the weather stays warm. When do you expect her home?"

Silence. Ruth saw his hat disappear. He was walking away. All she saw was the tip of the shovel lying on his shoulder before that, too, disappeared.

Ruth finished her lunch. Thomas jumped on the table and sniffed her plate. "Sorry, Thomas, nothing left for you," she said and carried her tray into the kitchen.

Josie Barrett was a talker, a widow like Ruth so they shared much in common. She was Ruth's other neighbor and she had joined Ruth for lunch. It was so quiet on the patio that Ruth could hear the sparrows chittering in the topmost branches of the cedar.

"Have you seen Didi?" Ruth asked as she served the ham salad. "I haven't heard her voice lately."

"Is she away again?" Josie smoothed the napkin on her lap. "She visits her sister quite often. Never known her to stay longer than a weekend."

"She sems to have been away for weeks," Ruth said. "Most days she calls over the fence and we have a little chat."

Josie Barrett and Didi Crow had known each other for years prior to Ruth buying her house. They were acquaintances, not friends, Josie had corrected her. They met at the supermarket or at the town library but they had never been inside each other's houses.

"That's odd." Josie gazed at the gray wooden fence. "I haven't seen her either. I've been so busy I've lost track of time."

Ruth finished the last of her salad. "He must be putting in new gardens. He's been fussing and digging, and I've heard him swearing. Really, Josie, how does Didi manage?" Ruth brought out a teacake warm from the oven.

Josie eyed the Crow's red tiled roof. "You think she's left him?" Josie dropped her voice. "That wouldn't surprise me."

"She's not happy?" Ruth guessed the answer. Maybe it wasn't their television she had heard on otherwise quiet evenings.

"She talked about it once, actually confided in me that Roger has a temper." Both women stared at the fence that separated the two houses. There was no sound coming from the Crow's garden. "You don't know what goes on behind anyone else's bedroom door, do you?" Josie brushed the crumbs of teacake from her napkin and waited for the sparrows to find them.

There was a moment of silence, and at that moment Thomas emerged from the hole under the fence and purred around Ruth's ankles. "Why, Thomas, where *has* your mistress gone?" Ruth patted his orange head and remembered the latest mystery she'd read. She knew about unhappy endings.

Ruth was enjoying her early morning cup of tea with the local newspaper when Thomas appeared. He was trailing a piece of fabric that was caught in his mouth, and she realized he had tried to swallow it but the cloth had caught in his throat.

Ruth picked him up. It was the first time she had held the cat, and his body was warm and heavy. She pulled the dirty strip of cloth from his mouth and Thomas coughed and struggled to free himself from her grip and then ran straight to the bowl of water by the back door and lapped greedily. The cloth was slippery, nylon, an old-lady pink. It reminded Ruth of her mother's nightgowns.

Ruth called Josie immediately and described the cloth Thomas had found. "You don't really think it could be Didi's?" Ruth was ashamed at the excitement in her voice. "If she isn't at her sister's place...?"

"Trust me, Ruth, nothing interesting ever happens on this street." Josie laughed. "You're letting your imagination run wild. Just let me know when you see her again."

Ruth didn't really know Didi beyond the occasional conversation over their shared fence. She thought she had heard her neighbors quarreling but it might have been the television, and the few times she had heard doors slamming it might have been caused by the wind. One never knew how couples lived their lives and Didi must have decided to stay with her sister for an extended holiday. Roger was not one to confide in his neighbor but the next time she heard Roger digging in his garden she'd ask for Didi's address, maybe send a note telling Didi she was missed and that the hummingbirds were still feeding at her fuchsia baskets.

Ruth poured a second cup of tea. In between sips, the Crow's old tomcat strolled through the hole in the fence. He jumped up on the opposite chair and waved his tail. Ruth felt a certain relief to see the animal. How easily, she thought, the mind devised a story out of nothing. How foolish to imagine that her neighbor could be burying anything other than compost.

The Carving Knife

My daughter held the knife at shoulder level, her two small hands wrapped around the wooden handle, the blade pointed at my waist. She was small and slight. Her head only came level with my chest. She was quivering with anger, and waves of animosity flowed forcefully from her taut little body. "No!" she said.

I stayed very still, arms at my side. No sudden moves, no attempt yet to take away the knife. It would be easier if she screamed or shouted. Her eyes, focused on mine, looked into and through me. The knife didn't waver. It was the kitchen knife I used for carving the tough meat or cutting up the root vegetables. She had seen me sharpen it just the other day. "Will it cut better?" she had asked then.

"Miss Taylor will be waiting for you,' I said evenly. "Your friends will be waiting, too." Foolishly I said friends instead of classmates.

She shifted her feet. "I don't have friends." The knife's tip caught on my cardigan. She swayed a little with the effort to keep the knife steady. There was sweat on her upper lip.

"But you like Miss Taylor," I said. The knife dipped in her hands. She was tiring.

Another time I had tried to take the knife, before she was ready to bargain, and she had cut my palm. She had watched the blood dribble down my wrist, held her breath and had fallen to the floor. These breath-holding episodes were quite frequent and always frightening.

I needed to be patient.

"I don't like school." The knife wavered. "You can't make me go."

"Maybe today," I said quietly. "We can make cookies." I heard rather than saw the intake of breath.

"I'd like that," she said, and the knife clattered to the floor. The moment had passed.

She leaned in against my body, waiting for my hug, and looked up into my face as though nothing unusual had occurred. Her eyes were bright with expectation. She loved chocolate-chip cookies.

I called this the knife-show when I told my husband that evening, stepping quickly over the details like it was a usual day.

The Winning Ticket

"Marion Ryan, #31," Mr. Parker called from the stage. The dandruff on the shoulders of his dark suit coat gleamed in the powerful overhead lights. He gave a little cough so the microphone screeched. He repeated my name and it came loud and clear over the heads of my parents and every neighbor I'd ever known in our small town.

"Marion Ryan, you here?"

People turned and smiled and shuffled like a herd of cows ready for milking.

My mother nodded her head for encouragement. "Go on," she hissed. "Go up and get it."

The bicycle sat up on the stage, apple red, with the chrome sweetly shined, and the seat black as the Bartlett's cat.

I fumbled in my pocket. You had to have the magic ticket, the one where you wrote your name in, the one stamped with 31 on it. You had to present it to Mr. Parker, from Parker's Department Store, in front of everyone. And you had to smile and smile, like I'd been coached by my mother. That was going to be easy because I was taking that bike home and I was showing it off this coming Sunday, riding down Wiggens Street with my pigtails flying.

"Marian Ann Ryan!"

"Go on," my mother said in a voice I understood. I scrambled out of my seat and flicked back my braids. My hands felt sticky. I held up the yellow square of paper with the 31 in thick black marker that was undeniable. "I'm here!" I called. "I'm here!"

"Come to the stage, dear," Mr. Parker smiled in encouragement. I heard the clapping. I heard Leonard Bradley mutter, "It's a set-up."

I stood deliberately on his foot as I passed between the seats, gratified to hear him gasp. "You don't get to ride it," I whispered.

"Drop dead!" he said.

That was the latest response to anything these days in my school, the most dreaded. It was like the double-dog dare I'd heard about from my brothers, but we were young and most things ran off our backs like water. Who could imagine such a thing, although Jackie Beston was shot dead last year when he and his friends were target shooting. Anything *could* happen but it only happened to others.

I walked up to the stage, up the three wooden steps, and smiled. Mr. Parker took my ticket and waved it above his head, while everyone below me clapped. Then I was holding the handlebars of the cherry-red bicycle and steering it carefully off the stage.

It was mine. It was the right color and I knew how to ride. I'd trained on my brothers' bikes with the top bar and fixed wheels.

This little beauty was a girl's bike and it had hand brakes for a downhill run. It was beautiful.

My father followed me out of the hall and lifted the bike up, into the back of our truck. I sat in the cab between my parents and smiled some more. I didn't care that my mother worked at Parker's, that maybe she'd swung a deal with Mr. Parker so the bike would come to me. I didn't care if Leonard thought he knew something. I was going to ride that bike to school every day and I was going to lock and chain it up so nobody could steal a ride.

The school days drifted on. Emily Madden's parents owned the local grocery store in town with a shelf lined with fat glass bottles filled with delicious lollies, and in my family, sweets were a luxury, allowed at birthdays and in Christmas stockings. Emily went home for lunch every day while I ate in the schoolyard with the other kids. It was a half mile walk to the shop, and by midday it was getting hot.

"Let me ride your bike home," Emily said. "And I'll bring you a gob-sucker."

A gob-sucker could last days if you managed it right. Each layer was a different color and as you sucked the layers were revealed. You could take it out of your mouth, wrap it in your handkerchief, keep it overnight, start another color the next day. They weren't allowed at school, so over a week the lolly acquired bits of lint and flecks of paper, but the taste was still there, and so were the beautiful changing colors.

I hesitated for a moment. "Don't you scratch it, Emily Madden!"

Emily mounted my cherry-red bike and rode off. Each day for a week, Emily borrowed my bike. At the end of the week, I had four gob-suckers stowed at the back of my panty drawer. Almost a year's supply if I sucked slowly or didn't choke to death. My brothers had shown me in graphic detail how someone choked, hands around their necks, tongues hanging out, eyes rolling round, so I didn't suck a gob-sucker in bed in case I fell asleep, choked, and died.

The next week we made the same bargain, but on Monday Emily was late returning to school and I watched as she jumped off the bike and threw it on the ground. That was that. Our deal was off. The cherry-red paint on the front mudguard was scratched. Several of the plastic "fliers" on the handlebars were torn off.

"You can't have it anymore," I said. I propped the bike on its metal stand.

"You don't get any more lollies," she said. "And I'll tell Mum you stole them."

That statement almost changed my mind, but the thought of her mother telling that lie to my mother was almost too much. Bella Madden was poison. She had a shrill voice and menacing big breasts and she made trouble for anyone in town who she felt had slighted her.

"I don't care." My bike meant more to me than the gobsuckers. "You don't borrow my bike again." There was mud stuck to the pedals where she'd thrown the bike to the ground and it had skidded for a bit.

Emily had two older brothers, both tall and thin, with shaggy blond hair. Eddie, the oldest, had a bit of hair on his cheeks which he bragged needed shaving every day. The other brother, Graham, was small for his age and he stood behind his older brother, ready to duck and run at the slightest hint of a fight. The next day, as I rode down the narrow path away from school, the boys were waiting for me. They were there where the track curved past the big wattle stand.

I could see Eddie was holding a long stick; Graham was crouched behind him in the long shivery grass. I pedaled faster but Eddie stepped forward. He pushed the stick through the spokes of the front wheel. The bike somersaulted. I was thrown off, my knees scraped the gravel and I heard the boys laughing as they ran off. My cherry-red bike lay on its side, its back wheel spinning, the front wheel spokes twisted out of shape.

How was I going to explain the gravel rash on my knees, bloodied and speckled from the tiny stones embedded in the skin. My dad might put the bike in the shed and say it was too dangerous for me to ride. He'd say, "Before you had the bike, you walked to school. You can walk again." Mother would put the dreaded Friar's Balsam on my injuries and that would hurt like hell.

It was while I was pulling the stick out of my wheel that I saw Jimmy Dawson heading down the school track. Jimmy was one of the big quiet boys who sat in the back row and couldn't write his name. He was slow but he was strong.

"You okay, Marion Ryan?" He stood with his hands hanging. He saw the blood on my knees and said, "What the *meffculuss*!" Jimmy sometimes did odd jobs around our farm and my father taught him that nonsense swear word to use instead of his usual stream of blasphemy. Jimmy loved the sound of the word as it rolled off his tongue.

"My wheel," I said. "It's broken."

"Nah," Jimmy lifted the bike. "Wheel's busted."

"Eddie put a stick through it," I said. I wanted to cry but in my family you only cried after someone died, you didn't waste tears on small things that could be fixed, like broken wheel spokes.

"I'll walk it home," I said. A trickle of blood had reached my white sock, and I was proud of that. It was a sign of tragedy, a very obvious sign.

I set the bike upright, and with the front wheel wobbling awkwardly, I set off for home. Jimmy walked beside me. When we reached the wide patch of sand at the base of Morton Hill where the water collected after rains, he took the bike and hoisted it onto his shoulders. I didn't need to thank him. My knees were really hurting by that time and I was relieved to have him take over.

When we reached my front gate, Jimmy handed over the bike and walked away. "Bye, Marion Ryan," he called back.

I endured the cotton wool saturated in Friar's Balsam, gritted my teeth, and said a bad word under my breath. My mother fussed and my father said he'd fix the bike that weekend so I'd have it come Monday.

On Monday the Madden boys stayed away from me and Emily stuck out her tongue when we were in line and the Head was lecturing us. I was glad to have something special that she wanted so I ignored her. That afternoon, Jimmy Dawson waited for me at the bend in the track. I slowed my pedaling and he walked beside me, long strides, and he said, "Madden kids," he said. "They brats!"

"I don't like the Maddens either," I said.

Jimmy took a long penknife out of his pocket. He took a flat stone out of his other pocket and spat on it. I stopped my bike and watched. He sharpened the blade on the wet stone, back and forth, back and forth. It was mesmerizing.

"Come on, Jimmy, I've gotta get home."

He wiped the blade down his pants and snapped the knife shut. "Okay, Emily Ryan." He cleared his throat and spat into the sand at his feet. "Those Madden kids give you trouble, I'm ready." And by the look on his face, I believed him. I knew he wasn't my friend, but he wouldn't hurt me, I knew that.

We were halfway to my home, beyond the sand patch where he carried my bike, when he left me and headed through the woods toward the back road. That's where he lived with a half dozen siblings and three rusted trucks.

On my way home the following week, Eddie and Graham jumped in front of my bike where the bend in the track obscured my sight. They made me swerve into the soft bank where my wheel caught in the tree roots. They howled and Eddie threw a stone at my leg. The red mudguard was stuck and I had to pull the handlebars hard to get it free. I was so intent on my new bike, I didn't see Jimmy Dawson come from behind the tall brush. I saw his penknife and the blade was out.

Events happened quickly. He grabbed Eddie by the back of his shirt and stabbed at his flailing arms and flung him in the grass where Graham let out a yelp. Jimmy grabbed the small brat and swung him out and into the sand patch, face down. I heard his body smack. There was blood on Eddie's sleeve and when Graham tried to stand there was blood coming from his nose.

"You go on home, Emily Ryan," Jimmy said as he stood over the Madden boys. "Won't trouble you no more."

I pedaled home as fast as I could. The streamers on my handlebars stayed limp even in the wind and the red mudguard sounded wobbly. I'd ask my brother to check my bike and fix the mudguard. I wouldn't bother my father this time in case he thought Jimmy was to blame or the red bike was the problem and put it up in the shed rafters. I wasn't going to tell anyone what happened. I didn't want Jimmy Dawson getting in trouble for helping me, and knowing Jimmy was protecting me meant the Madden kids wouldn't bother me ever again.

Coming Home

The house was dark when I arrived at the family farm. Even the kitchen lights were out, which was strange because everyone lived their days beside the wood-stove in that room, the center of family activity, the room where our mother reigned supreme. I hadn't seen my folks in a year, and this visit home was meant to be a surprise, their first-born daughter returning after months of travel. It was a clear fall afternoon when I arrived, and the stand of white birch beside the house was decked out in glorious late-September color.

I knocked. Funny, I thought, I've never knocked before, so I waited a moment before I turned the knob. The kitchen was dark but there was enough light from the front windows to see my father was sitting at the head of the kitchen table, just sitting, no cigarette in his mouth, hands resting on the table. He's praying, I thought. Something's happened. Where was mother?

With my brightest smile I said, "Hello Dad, I'm home at last," and I switched on the light. I put my duffel bag on the floor, dusty and shapeless from being strapped to the backseat of my motor scooter. I had been traveling around the White Mountains on my Heinkel, staying with various friends from my college days, and waiting to start a new job in Boston.

My father looked up, his face lightened. "Jennie, is that you?" He didn't get up. "Were we expecting you?" He started to rise, but slowly, as though his legs were not taking his weight. "Is Annie with you?"

There was little warmth in the room and I wondered how long my father had been sitting there. There was wood by the stove but there was no heat so I stoked the still-red coals and put on some wood.

"Annie's in Vermont, dad. I've been traveling."

"We weren't expecting you." He pointed at the kettle. "Now you're here, Jen, you might make a cup of tea for us."

I filled the big kettle and swung it onto the woodstove where mother had cooked a thousand meals. I packed in some more wood to get the fire heating again. I had warmed up before that woodstove all through my childhood, my cold hands out to catch the heat, inhaling the rich cooking smells. Mother would nudge me aside, oven cloth in her hands, pulling casseroles out of the oven or catching up the prepared soup pot. The woodstove was the warm center of the room and it was here that mother was undeniably in charge.

The kettle whistled. The cannister of tea sat next to an empty cannister marked coffee. That canister had always been empty, yet it was allowed to stay because it was part of a set received as a wedding gift to my parents. I brought two cups and their matching saucers to the table and my father pulled the sugar bowl near his cup.

“Where’s Mum gone?” I asked.

Through the kitchen window the rhododendrons were bare of flowers and I remembered how the spider webs strung across the branches caught the dew, how when I was a child I broke the webs with a stick and watched the spider silently scuttle for cover. A week ago, I was coming down from Conway and the morning air was scented fresh. On the downward slope of the white mountain, I scattered a flock of black crows that rose up from the creek, a furious flapping of wings, their disturbed cries echoing.

“She’s visiting friends.” He sipped the tea. “You know how she likes to visit her friends.” His knuckles were so large he could barely hold the teacup. “That tastes good, Jen. I’m glad you’re here.”

I filled his cup again. “So, what are you having for dinner, Dad?” The fire had been stoked and gave out some warmth but there was nothing heating on the stove top. Mother usually had a soup pot on the back of the stove, something in the oven slow baking, but the kitchen was squeaky clean, the counters bare. “How long has Mum been away?”

“A day or two.” He rubbed his eyes.

I was tired from the trip, but my father looked exhausted. His shoulders were slumped, and his hair was tousled. He looked like he hadn’t showered today, like he hadn’t slept much either. He was in his work clothes. Usually, he washed up for supper and shed his work boots outside the back door.

“How long are you staying, Pet?”

“Not long. I start the new job in Boston next week.” I waited for him to ask me about my plans, but his eyes were focused on his teacup.

He looked up and said, “You can sleep in the guest room.”

The guest room? That was my childhood bedroom. Had I been away so long that he thought of me as a guest? I picked up my bag. "I'll wash up and then I'll get some supper."

"Good idea." He was rolling a cigarette, tobacco lined up on the small slip of rice paper, a swift graze of his tongue, finished with an expert roll into a cylinder. He lit his smoke and gazed off at the closed back door as though I wasn't there.

The bathroom was at the end of the back verandah. A mop stood in a bucket, half-filled with gray water. My mother had obviously left it there in mid-mopping, just walked away. I wondered what could have disturbed her usual routines, what would bring her to leave the cleaning unfinished? The verandah held the wooden box that was filled with wood for the kitchen fire. It was half-empty. The wood-stove in the kitchen stayed on all day and into the evening. It was the heat for the house. The wood heap lay close by, beyond the stone wall where the compost collected and crows in the early morning gathered to fight over the food scraps. My father usually kept the wood box filled, that was his daily job, the collecting of firewood so Mother could cook the family meals and keep the house warm.

I went through to the guest room where the floral wallpaper still covered the walls, bunches of roses tied with blue ribbons. There were brown streaks in the corner where water damage happened years ago and Annie and I had made up stories out of the markings, lying in twin beds under quilts mother had made. Even though Annie and I had left home, it would always be our room, our childhood bedroom. I wished Annie was there and wondered why I hadn't asked her to come home while I was visiting. We could have had a reunion before I started work. We could have seen Mum and Dad before we left home again.

The stove was heating the kitchen nicely when I returned.

“So, Mother’s in New York?” I asked. Mother’s relatives were numerous and every so often she would announce at the breakfast table that she was going on a visit. “I need a few days away,” she’d say, and our father would take her to catch the New York-bound train the next morning. She always returned from those trips animated and full of family gossip.

My father looked at me and smiled. “Who are you, dear?” His eyes were bloodshot, tired, but he had the sweetest smile that moved upwards from his mouth into his blue eyes.

I looked to see if he was joking, but he seemed puzzled. He put his cup down carefully and lit another cigarette. “We weren’t expecting anyone today.”

“Dad,” I said. “I’m Jennie, your daughter, Jennie.” When did he get so old, I wondered.

There was a moment, as the smoke spiraled up from his smoke, that I thought, he doesn’t know who I am. Then his eyes focused.

“Ah, Jennie. I’m glad you’re home.”

“I’ll make us some supper.” I put more wood on the fire. I searched the cupboard for some bread, some of Mum’s homemade jam and I found half a loaf and a half empty jar of blueberry jam. Little more. It seemed no one had gone shopping, which was strange as my parents had their routines, shopping every Friday at the All Goods Shop in the next town.

“She went away.” My father fumbled for his matches. I realized some things hadn’t changed, he was still using Redheads to light his cigarettes. “We’d better have supper, Pet. Just make a sandwich, that will do.”

I made the sandwiches and poured another cup of black tea. My father ate the sandwich in large mouthfuls, chewing and swallowing between sips. He looked like a man who hadn’t eaten in days. I made another sandwich and he ate that, too.

"You need to get to bed," I said.

"I'm sleeping on the verandah. I can't sleep in the bedroom now." He stood, pulling himself up and straightening his back, and he looked at me. "Ah!, you've come home, Jennie," he said. "When did you get here?"

"It's okay dad, I'm home now for a few days." I took his arm like I might a child and led him through the living room and out to the side verandah where Annie and I had slept in the hot summer weeks, reading adventure books in the summer holidays and listening to the barn owl's call as we drifted off to sleep.

"Where's Annie?" he asked.

"She's in Burlington, Dad, you know, studying."

His pajamas were there, in a heap on the bed. "I can manage," he said. So, I left him struggling out of his sweater and went to check the kitchen stove. I was puzzled. Why would he be sleeping out on the verandah? It didn't make sense. Once fall arrived it was too chilly to sleep out there. I checked to see if he had enough blankets and straightened the old blue and white quilt Annie and I once used to make a hiding place among the chairs.

I went through to my parents' bedroom and the door was shut. The door had never been shut except when they were asleep or to keep us children out. It was their private space. The house was so still. So quiet. I could smell lilacs, so faint I couldn't place the scent at first. Years ago, mother had planted three lilac bushes by the front gate, the old-fashioned variety that bloomed twice a year, in spring and again in the fall, deep purple in color and sweet smelling.

Why wasn't my father sleeping where he always slept? When Mother visited family in New York, he slept there, he never slept on the verandah. I opened the door slowly. There was enough light from the large front windows to see that Mother was there. She lay flat in bed with their faded patchwork quilt neatly tucked around her. At first glance I thought she was sleeping, but no, not as quiet as this, not without breath, not with her hair in such disarray on the pillow. On the bedside table my father had placed a large vase of purple lilacs, drooping now and browning, my mother's favorite flowers.

Mud Season

"Well, what do you know?" I turned my chair to watch the pigeons strutting along the ledge outside my office on the sixth floor and there he was. "Hey Sam, come look. Henry's having a smoke out on the ledge again."

Sam and I shared office space with Henry Littleman at a branch office of Boyle Insurance Company in Boston.

"How many times has he done it this year?" I asked. Sam barely raised his head from his computer.

We'd all smoked on the ledge from time to time, a rite of passage of sorts. Hadn't I been out there just last year smoking a cigarette with Sam shouting out to "Give it up, Spencer, get a life. You'll be playing golf in no time!" It was the thought of golf that did it, the smell of fresh-mown grass, the possibility of a hole-in-one. I had never hit an eagle and the possibility of that happening had made me come in. I had at down then and written the best damn insurance claim ever.

"I tell you, Sam, we should do something. Look how close he is to the edge."

Sam grunted.

"He's scaring the pigeons Sam. Look at them. Poor damned birds don't know who's come to join them."

Of the four large windows facing the street, we had two windows in our department for pigeon gazing and weather watching. Fifty yards away there were two more windows for Watson's Modern Design space. We were two separate entities, the room divided up by moveable walls. Her team was so busy they were unaware of Henry standing outside our windows.

Henry was smoking. I could see his square-toed shoes resting on the twenty-four-inch concrete ledge. Only a fool would wear those flashy tan loafers this time of year. Not a good advertisement for the most successful insurance business in the city. But then I wondered: What if Henry wasn't such a fool? What if he was depressed? We were in the middle of mud season, and everyone experienced the seasonal blues.

I opened the window a few more inches and a cool wind rushed in. "Whatever it is, Henry," my voice was gentle, "It will pass."

I knew the feeling. Every year mud season arrives with gray skies and slushy streets. The kids all have colds, our wives are miserable from the grayness, our cars are cranky. We had all joked in the office at some point about jumping from the ledge, but it was just joking, just like we all prayed for sunny days, leafed-out trees and a mild allergy season.

"The wind's really cold out there, Henry, you need to smoke downstairs, have some coffee, get warm again."

"I'm not coming in." Henry's voice trailed off.

"What are you talking about? You can't stay out there." This was unlike Henry. I wondered if I should call a counselor, someone professional. "You really need to come in, Henry."

"This time I'm going to jump. No one's had the guts before." Henry inhaled and slowly released a gray-blue stream of smoke. "I can hit the net, hit the bullseye, I know I can."

"Those bets were just office talk, passing the time." I said, "No one bet on hitting the bullseye. We were just kidding around."

How many times had we placed bets in the coffee lounge that someone who made the decision to jump from the ledge would hit the net six floors below? And hit that tiny bullseye? Never! We even joked about who'd call the fire department. It was never meant to be taken seriously, just gallows humor to get through the week. But I often wondered who would have the nerve to collect the money supposing the unthinkable happened and the jumper missed the net.

But Henry bet that anyone could jump and hit the net. On a clear day, without any wind, he bet he could hit the bullseye. He'd collect the winnings and be a hero, too. Everyone laughed at the idea.

The wind caught the side of Henry's hair and lifted it like a small dark wing. I shouldn't worry. He seemed solid enough. He worked at his desk like we all did, family photos beside his computer, a bobble-head of Tom Brady alongside. Henry was safe, he was just taking a break, he was out on the ledge and he'd be in soon, because no one seriously thinks of jumping. Life just gets to you sometimes, so you need to clear your head, have time away from computer screens, the constant buzz of conversation, the competition.

Sam closed his computer and came over to my desk. "That's it, Spencer, he's playing us. Let's ask Henry if he wants the firemen called now." Sam had been sucking on licorice straps again and his breath was musty. "It could go national, a story like this, man on a ledge." Sam was hamming it up. "Not a nice thing for your mother to see on TV." His voice was squeaky high like he'd sucked in helium.

Now why would Sam think of Henry's mother in Florida? Sure, Henry had mentioned she'd been in hospital, that he couldn't take time off to visit her, but it was Henry's wife and kids who would be impacted the most.

I'd met Henry's wife at the Christmas party, and she was blonde and wispy while Henry was tall and thin. I wondered how they managed, both divorced and giving marriage a second chance. Blended families took energy and compromise, and they ended up with five kids between them. I hadn't thought of asking him how family life was going. You get busy with work and forget your colleagues have mortgages and personal lives.

"Spencer, ask Henry what he thinks, which channel he might have a preference for?" Sam was waiting to see if Henry was listening.

"Let it go, Sam, he's just resting up." I pushed the window higher and leaned through. "Hey, Henry!" Two pigeons flew up with a racket of wings. Henry gazed straight ahead. "You okay to come in now?" I asked. "I'll get you some coffee, its chilly out there."

"March is a rotten time of year," Henry said. His loafers sported little leather tassels. He was still smoking, one hand lifting the cigarette to his mouth, the other hand flat against the building, steadying himself against the wind.

"You want anything?" I asked again. "You want more privacy?" I wondered if anyone on Elizabeth Street was looking up, watching him, six stories above.

Henry was somewhat shielded by the buttress that separated one section of the building from the other. Only our window was open. The windows at Watson's Design beyond the buttress were closed, and her staff hadn't noticed Henry out on the ledge yet.

"Look Henry, it'll be May soon. Longer days, more light. Golf courses greening up." I tried to sound reassuring. Henry's jacket looked thin for this time of year.

Sam pushed me away from the window. "Let me try," he whispered. His hands were white-knuckled on the windowsill. "So, what's up, Henry?" The story was that Sam had been out on the ledge when he was new to the firm, but I hadn't witnessed it. "You can't stay out any longer, Henry. You'll freeze. Then you'll fall." His voice was firm. "Finish your smoke and come on in."

A pigeon tapped along the ledge toward Henry's shoes. I saw the arc of his cigarette, spitting tiny sparks as it fell through the air. Henry coughed several times but didn't reply.

We waited a few more seconds then Sam straightened at the window and turned to me. "He's not listening, Spencer, he's all tense," he squinted against the light. "I don't like it. You better call 911!"

My cell phone was on the desk. "No need calling," Sam said, once again looking out the window. "I can hear sirens now. Someone must have called it in." His shoulders were hunched against the frame. "You hear those sirens, Henry, the whole damn street is watching."

I nudged Sam aside and watched as the police drove up, the fire trucks, gawkers were gathering, possibly some reporters. The firemen in their yellow suits brought out the net and I saw the bullseye. How could anyone think of falling, expecting to find that little black dot?

"Henry," I said firmly. "It's a long way down and there's no guarantee you'll make it."

"You can start taking bets, Spencer," he said.

"For God's sake, Henry, get a hold of yourself!" Why hadn't I asked more about his wife, about how his kids were doing? "You know we were joking, Henry. Really!"

Sam tugged my jacket. He was sweating. "He's going to do it, Spencer! Tell him he'll be on TV and his mother will see it. Down in Florida, she'll see him fall." And I wondered again why Sam thought of Henry's mother first rather than Henry's wife? I realized I didn't know either of my co-workers, didn't know who they really were or what worried them.

Henry faced into the wind; his coat was blowing out from his body.

"Your mother...," I began.

Sam pushed me away from the window. "Listen, Henry!" He paused, then, "Oh my God!" I caught Sam as he fell against me and onto the floor. "He jumped!" Sam whispered. His face was chalky white and sweat beaded his upper lip.

"Did they catch him?" I asked. "Sam, did they?"

I leaned further out the window. I saw people running, people hugging each other, people pointing up at our windows, flashbulbs firing. I watched as firemen in yellow jackets carried a stretcher off toward the open ambulance doors and I thought I saw a raised hand, a little wave. It was Henry, I was sure of it, and he was alive.

I felt a sudden rush of adrenaline. This year I didn't have the nerve to ante up when we were all joking around in the coffee room, laying bets as to who might jump this mud season, who'd break in March, who'd be most likely to hit the black dot when the firemen unrolled the net. Even when Henry joked that if it was him that was jumping, he'd make damn sure he hit the bullseye. And here he was falling from six floors up hitting the net *smack* dead center. I could only imagine he fell with his eyes closed so it must have been dumbblind luck.

Sam struggled up off the floor. "Can you believe it, Spencer? Henry did what he promised he'd do."

"You've got to call his family, Sam," I said. I wondered if the local television network had made it in time. Should Sam tell his mother to watch the Boston news tonight? And Henry's wife? She should know her husband had jumped from six floors up, hit the bullseye, and survived the odds. Tomorrow everyone will be reading the headlines. Henry's face and name will be front page in all the supermarkets.

By this time Diane Watson and her staff were at their windows buzzing with excited conversation. "Did you see it? Did they catch him?" A chorus of voices! "Did they catch it on TV? Who was it that jumped?"

I sat down slowly at my desk; my legs wouldn't hold me up. Who could believe it? I hadn't placed a single bet in the coffee room even though I'd heard what Henry had said, the conviction in his voice. I hadn't pegged Henry Littleman for this sort of hero.

The N.J. Book Club

Fort Lee, New Jersey: It was 1973, six months since I, an Australian, had arrived in America with my husband and small son. We were living in a high-rise apartment block and I knew nobody in New Jersey so I spent many hours reading and knitting in a nearby park while my son was at school. One day, an American woman introduced herself and we became friends over the authors we admired. Sometime later, she invited me to join her book club.

I have forgotten the first book we discussed, it went by in a blur of introductions and newness. It was my second meeting with this New Jersey book group that I remember vividly. We were handed the book *Nigger*, an autobiography by Dick Gregory, and the designated leader handed out paper and pencils to each member. She asked us to divide the page and write *Black* on one side at the top, *White* on the other. She asked us to make a list of all the words or phrases generated by the two words. I wrote my lists and for the first time really thought about those associations. The list under *Black* was all dark and dangerous, under *White* it was all purity and goodness.

I was alternately energized and bewildered by the ideas and comments of the women who knew so much more about the world than I did. Dick Gregory's story fascinated me. Years ago, in Canberra, I saw books in the university bookstore with photos of the Ku Klux Klansmen gathered at rallies, their white robes, black slits for eyes. I saw photos of negroes hanging from trees, of burning houses and mobs and marches. I knew of Martin Luther King, had read Baldwin's "Fire Next Time." I understood "nigger" was a derogatory term and that negroes or black Americans were considered second-class citizens. I had no concept of how their lives were lived, how bitter their daily experiences were in the seventies in America.

Never once did I associate the conditions of the American negroes with the conditions of our indigenous people, the Australian Aborigine. Nor had I questioned the strongly entrenched view in white Australia that citizens who were black, i.e. "Abos" were inferior. While I was growing up, Australia enforced a "White Australia" policy until 1973.

In New Jersey, the book *Nigger* was discussed with great emotion. The women sympathized, argued, were horrified by some of the details, assured that we, in this room, could never treat black Americans the way Dick Gregory was treated. And yet, there we were, eight comfortably educated women and not a black American in the group. And how many black Americans did I know at that time? None?

How pleasant it was for me to be in that beautiful apartment with the soft sofas and padded chairs, the silver coffee urn, the polished tongs beside the bowl of sugar cubes. I understood nothing. I was like a child standing outside the door of the parents' bedroom late at night, wondering at the sounds I heard.

We had come to the end of the discussion, our books were closed, *Nigger* was in the forefront of our minds yet nicely distanced in the soft lamplight. We were relaxing over our porcelain coffee cups.

I heard one woman's voice rise. She was one of the most outspoken. She was speaking about the Jewish situation in Israel, the Yom Kippur War, an Arab Israeli war. Her friends were collecting money to send back to the "homeland" and she asked that everyone in the room become involved, to write checks. There were murmurs of agreement. I looked at the other women, really looked at them. They were all dark-haired, olive-complexioned, attractive and alive. For the first time I realized they were all Jewish. My friend was Jewish. Why hadn't I seen it before? They were united in their cause and I was the outsider.

I had known only one Jew in Australia, my cousin's husband. I had heard the whispers around their wedding. How his family escaped from Germany and how they finally reached Australia. He was a calm, lovely man and the only family member to speak at my father's funeral.

"Those fucking Protestants are responsible for everything!" the woman said, anger layering her words, so they hung in the air. She talked of the wasps and something to do with their lack of support. I thought it was perhaps the government she was blaming, the white liberals fault, an American fault.

She had a sympathetic audience, and I remembered seeing a headline in a New Jersey newspaper about the Israeli War, but it was light-years away from me, a newly arrived Australian. Then the woman repeated the earlier phrase about the waspy

Protestants and her face was flushed with emotion.

I heard a teaspoon rattling in a saucer. Silver against porcelain. The hot coffee in my cup splashed on my hand. It was my teaspoon making the noise. I looked around to see if anyone had heard, and when no one noticed, I placed my cup and saucer and the offending teaspoon on the table.

The women were animated and focused but I didn't hear their words. Couldn't hear them, for I had in that moment realized I was the outsider in the room, the minority, the fucking Protestant. And I wondered if I was also a wasp, and what it meant, this reference to a yellow-bellied stinging insect.

Later that night I tried to explain to my husband what had occurred. I had shared, however briefly, some alliance with Dick Gregory. I was not personally harassed. I was not afraid for my life. I had not been asked to leave the room, but I knew I was the outsider there. Fifty years after the event I carry a reminder of that moment like a string tied tightly to my forefinger, the rattle of a teaspoon against a fragile saucer.

Charlie Woods

I was fourteen when Charlie Woods ran down the riverbank with his arms raised and dived headfirst into the Matchem River. I remember the afternoon was filled with the hot smell of the bush, when the golden light sifted through the leaves of the ghost gums and shadows fell on the damp sand. It had rained in the past week, so everyone welcomed the sun and the call of cicadas in the yellow wattle trees. Charlie was my first love. We were in our middle-school years, when life was full of possibility and the innocence of young friendship.

Charlie was one of the Barnardo boys from Braywood Park Home. He was one of the homeless boys, lifted from the streets of post-war London by Dr. Barnardo and shipped to Australia after the Second World War. They were displaced children, far from home, orphaned when their parents were killed during the bombing of London or deserted during those war-torn years.

They filled the classrooms of my middle school with their cockney speech and their strange street slang.

Charlie played center on the school's football team, and he was the reason Williston High carried off every pennant in the region that year. He was only fifteen, but he played the game as though he'd been born with a ball in his hands. With his snub-nose and freckles, his carrot-colored hair flaming in the sun, he'd lean his body into the wind as he flew down the field. During one game he dislocated his shoulder, and when the bodies were peeled off him, he held the ball so tightly it had to be pried from the crook of his arm.

That last spring, the spring before I was sent off to a private school in Sydney, he rode ten miles from Braywood to see me. When he arrived at the family farm, my father suggested Charlie could earn some money by picking fruit that day. When the mid-morning break came, my mother called my father and brother into the house for tea, and I was called to join them. Charlie was not invited. I watched him through the kitchen window where he remained outside with the other men and their ragtag families, the itinerant workers who labored for the farmers in town.

One Saturday afternoon after the regional football competition had finished, and about a month after his visit to the farm, Charlie rode out to see me again. The day was unseasonably hot. He said the steep slope of Wilson Hill was the worst part of the ride, but the rest had been a breeze. He had tied his brown sweater between the handlebars and somewhere along the way one sleeve had caught in the wheel spokes and the cuff had been ripped off.

My parents were off visiting friends, so Charlie and I wandered round the farm until I suggested we ride to the local campground. The campground was a burned-out sand patch set among gum trees with an uninteresting little creek meandering among the rocks. Once we had walked the perimeter and thrown rocks into the creek there was nothing else to do. It was Charlie who suggested we ride on, so we turned our bikes toward the next small town.

It was a longer ride than we had imagined so I was glad to stop at the little store there for a bottle of water. I remember how exhausted I felt, the dragging pain in my leg muscles, but I could never admit it was all a mistake. That it had been too long a ride. There were no streetlights back then and very few houses along the road. I stumbled many times as we pushed our bikes up Wilson Hill, and once Charlie offered to push my bike, but I couldn't let him do that, his breathing was as ragged as mine.

When we arrived home it was dark and my father's truck, with its headlights full on, was pulling out of the garage. Charlie and I were exhausted. My hands were slipping off the handlebars and my legs barely supported the dragging weight of my body. My father leapt from the truck, tore the bike from my grasp, and wheeled it quickly into the shed. He didn't look at me and his voice was sharp when he told me to go into the house. I walked past my mother who, without a word, pointed me to my bedroom. I didn't hear what was said to Charlie.

The event was never mentioned again. It was days later before I wondered if my usually kind father had sent an exhausted boy off into the night, or whether he had relented and driven him there, but I doubted that. I knew it was more than a concern for my safety. It was about Charlie being a Barnardo boy, about Charlie being left alone to eat his lunch out by the side of the shed.

Some weeks later it was time for the Braywood boys' yearly dance. They were carefully chaperoned affairs, and I remembered the huge dining room looped with pale pink streamers, the bare waxed floor and the straight-backed chairs set side-by-side around the room. There was nothing to soften the drabness of the brown walls except the huge Union Jack flag tacked up behind the stage. The boys hung about in small groups near the doors, grinning and pointing and nudging each other, while the girls in their bright party dresses clustered near the record player.

I waited all evening for Charlie to enter the hall, but he never did. I danced with his friends instead and when I asked after Charlie, they told me Charlie didn't know how to dance, that he had the flu, that he'd strained a leg muscle and couldn't put his foot to the ground. Everyone gave a different excuse.

The school year was nearly over. Although I saw Charlie every day, we never spoke to each other again. Cricket had overtaken football. Every Wednesday afternoon the boys played cricket matches on the town field, and my girlfriends and I watched Charlie send the red ball straight as a die toward the central stump, fast and deadly, the school's top bowler. After the game was over and the teachers had gone, everyone walked down to the Matcham River. The river ran through a grove of gentle she-oaks and the Barnardo boys swam there with the local boys. They brought their swimming trunks rolled up in towels and hidden in the bottom of their satchels. They'd been warned that the river was dangerous. The riverbed moved as the summer storms swept down the valley and sandbars were present one day and gone the next, but those warnings didn't stop them.

Not everyone swam. We girls leaned over the metal footbridge, laughing and calling out to the boys below. The river was too gritty, too muddy for us, so we were there to watch the boys show off their young bodies. The Braywood boys were always the first to wade in, the ones who saw it all as a joke, a way of lengthening the freedom of those afternoons.

It was Charlie who first tested the waters of the Matcham River on that lush, summer-hot day in early November. They were celebrating the win against Pendleton Academy. It was Charlie who raced the length of the riverbank, who raised his hands in a mock salute of victory, who dived straight as an arrow into the water.

There was a sudden splash before the water settled. It took a moment before anyone realized he hadn't surfaced. Someone screamed. The boys in the water froze until someone pulled him up from the cloudy waters. We girls clung to each other and watched as his body was hauled onto the muddy bank. I remember the siren's wail and how small Charlie looked, his red hair slicked back and darkened by the river water.

They said he was paralyzed from the neck down, a quadriplegic. His neck bones had been crushed. School friends visited him in the hospital during the Christmas holidays, and they said he was in good spirits; he didn't need the respirator anymore; he could talk again. I asked my parents if I could visit him, but my parents said it was too far, too long a trip to the hospital, the farm was too busy for my father to get away and my mother didn't drive.

Charlie's accident happened in another life, but seven decades later, I remember the details clearly: the sweat on his young body as he ran down the bank, the joyous moment as he dived into the river, the red hair shifting on the water, the limp brown cotton shorts, and the sudden scream that parted some girl's lips.

The Christmas Wreath

I saw the truck ahead of me was slowing. It had snowed the past two days, and the roads were icy, so I thought at first there was an accident up ahead, that maybe a car had hit some black ice and slid off the road. It was Christmas Eve and I was on my way to my sister's house for supper. My gifts were on the back seat, a newly baked quiche in a carryall on the floor, wrapped gifts for everyone tied with red raffia bows.

The truck in front of me had Casella printed in large green letters across the back of the cab. It was a garbage truck and leaking out from under its curved back were sheets of cardboard and white plastic bags that fluttered in the wind.

I checked that my windows were wound up in my little car, that the heater was on. I'd worked later than I'd planned, and I knew my phone wouldn't have service out here so I couldn't call and let the family know I was going to be late. I imagined the fire lit and a Christmas tree laden with ornaments, gifts waiting under the tree, turkey browning in the oven.

Then I saw the animal. It was a moose, standing like some primordial statue on the other side of the road, shaggy, gaunt and looming large. Cars on both lanes, coming and going, were not moving, and their headlights lit up the stationary animal. Everyone was waiting for the moose to cross the road, but he wasn't moving.

To my surprise, a young man jumped down from the Casella's cab and walked to the back of the truck, his green uniform lit by my headlights. He seemed to be searching for something, but I couldn't see clearly. He straightened, and he had something quite large in his hands. He walked slowly across the road, with his shadow bobbing behind him, then in front, growing and shrinking in the headlights.

I held tightly to the steering wheel. My heart was thumping over the sound of my car idling. Like everyone else, I guessed we were waiting for the moose to charge.

The guy was holding something that looked like a small tire. It was hard to see against the headlights; those new halogens are blinding. The guy slowed, seemed to be moving his head, maybe talking, or shouting to the moose, who knew?

"Don't be brave!" I wanted to yell. "Moose are dangerous!" Living in New England we'd all heard stories of charging moose and the unpleasant aftermath. My hands were sweating, and the wheel was slippery. The car was heating up and I wanted to shed my coat, but I couldn't move.

The moose took a step forward. It lowered its shaggy head, and I could see its breath against the darkness of the trees. Its antlers were great bony things, branching out from its head. It looked like an old one, unsettled by the lights and the noise of many motors. It was majestic though, stately, and the Casella man in his green uniform was dwarfed by its bulk.

I could make out the gold circle surrounding the Casella logo on the back of his jacket, and I thought how odd it was to be registering these details when there could be a killing right in front of us. The cars on the other side of the road were stationary. Not one car moved. Not one driver hit their horn or called out. It seemed everyone was waiting.

Then the Casella guy lifted his arm, and I saw that the small tire was really a large green wreath with a trail of little red and silver bobbles floating off its edges, festive eye-candy caught in the headlights.

He balanced elegantly on his toes, a matador poised before the kill, and threw the wreath over the foremost antlers, a huge throw, high and well placed. The wreath landed and the moose shook its head gently, surprised by the sudden weight. The wreath stayed, caught in place. The trail of little colored lights slanted down its neck like small jewels.

"Wow!" I thought. What a story I had to tell my sister.

The moose raised its head. I think everyone was holding their collective breaths, stunned by what had just happened. It was unexpected, awesome in the true sense of the word. The Casella guy walked back to his truck and swung up into its cab. He was safe, and I realized I had been dreading another sort of outcome.

Horns began honking up and down the length of traffic, headlights flashed, it was a collective chorus of relief.

And only then, amid all the applause, the moose walked slowly, majestically, across the road, its head erect, and the wreath settled like a large green crown on its massive antlers. It was as though the animal understood the timing, the part it played in a timeless Christmas pageant.

Other short story collections
by Geraldine M. North:

Butcher Bird: Tales from Down Under
26 short stories that capture the universal aspects of the human experience within the peculiar ethos of rural Australia.

The Empty Bird Cage: Short Stories
19 stories that examine contemporary life, primarily in the United States.

Available at Amazon.com and elsewhere.

Acknowledgments

I was born in Australia, came to the United States in 1972, and with my husband and two children, settled in Hanover, New Hampshire. My first book of short stories, "Butcher Bird" was published in 2016. My second book, "The Empty Birdcage" was published in 2019.

This third book of short stories was completed in Bryan, Texas.

"Dancing Girls" would not be possible without the love and support of my family and friends, and to the professional support of Deborah Heimann of Tiny Tremors, and the talent of Jeffrey Zygmont of Free People Publishing.

www.ingramcontent.com/pod-product-compliance
Lightning Source LLC
LaVergne TN
LVHW051005080826
845145LV00009B/2463

* 9 7 8 1 9 3 4 5 8 2 8 9 3 *